The Cupcaked Crusader to the rescue?

Horace knew he had to act fast. He stuffed the Celernip Festival announcement in his pocket and raced behind a bush. From inside his backpack, he took out a purple taffeta suit and a small aluminum ball containing one special afterschool treat.

The Cupcaked Crusader would save all of them.

Horace slipped his costume over his clothes and unwrapped the ball of foil. It contained a new type of cupcake his sister had baked last week. It had a green cake bottom and top with a layer of horseradish frosting in the middle. His sister didn't usually give him cupcakes for the fun of it, so Horace had had to beg her for one and promise to wash and iron her Lily Deaver Scout uniforms every afternoon for a month.

Horace shoved the piece of cake in his mouth and began chewing.

Immediately, he felt as if something had gone terribly, terribly wrong. Melody's superpower-giving cupcakes had never made him feel as weird as this before. . . .

Horace Splattly
THE CUPCAKED CRUSADER

The Terror of the Pink Dodo Balloons

by **Lawrence David**

illustrated by **Barry Gott**

PUFFIN BOOKS

For Marc David,
my one-year-younger brother, who once drove my
mother's car around town with a pet boa
constrictor hanging around his neck, and then
when he left the snake in the car, it crawled up
under the dashboard and wouldn't come out

—*L.D.*

PUFFIN BOOKS
Published by the Penguin Group
Penguin Putnam Books for Young Readers,
345 Hudson Street, New York, New York 10014, U.S.A.
Penguin Books Ltd, 80 Strand, London WC2R ORL England
Penguin Books Australia Ltd, 250 Camberwell Road, Camberwell, Victoria 3124, Australia
Penguin Books Canada Ltd, 10 Alcorn Avenue, Toronto, Ontario, Canada M4V 3B2
Penguin Books (N.Z.) Ltd, 182-190 Wairau Road, Auckland 10, New Zealand
Penguin Books Ltd, Registered Offices: Harmondsworth, Middlesex, England

Published simultaneously by Dutton Children's Books and Puffin Books,
divisions of Penguin Putnam Books for Young Readers, 2003

1   3   5   7   9   10   8   6   4   2

THE LIBRARY OF CONGRESS HAS CATALOGED THE DUTTON EDITION AS FOLLOWS:
David, Lawrence.
Horace Splattly, the Cupcaked Crusader: the terror of the pink dodo balloons /
by Lawrence David; illustrated by Barry Gott.—1st ed.   p.   cm.
Summary: Little Horace Splattly, alias the Cupcaked Crusader, hopes to
become Celernip Prince at the Celernip Festival, keep his best friends, win
the love of Sara Willow, cope with his talented scientist sister, and figure
out who is creating the pink dodo balloons that are making people bald.
ISBN 0-525-46867-6
[1. Heroes—Fiction. 2. Festivals—Fiction. 3. Contests—Fiction. 4. Friendship—Fiction.
5. Size—Fiction. 6. Humorous stories.] I. Gott, Barry, ill. II. Title.
PZ7.D28232 Ho 2003   [Fic]—dc21   2002074144

Puffin Books ISBN 0-14-250001-1
Printed in the United States of America

Contents

Chapter 1

STILL THE SHORTEST FOURTH GRADER IN ALL OF BLOOTINVILLE

Mr. Dienow stood behind his desk at the front of the classroom. He scowled at the class of fourth-grade students. The tall, skinny teacher pulled on his pointy beard with one hand and poked the tip of a metal ruler at the large, twisted bone that lay on his desk. "Can't *anyone* in the class tell me what kind of creature this belongs to?" he asked.

Silence.

"No one knows?" Dienow asked, his face growing as red as the tomatoes in the cafeteria's hot tomato ice cream. "This may be the last day of the school year, but I promise that no one is leaving this room until I get an answer!" He lifted his ruler and flung it across the room.

All the kids ducked. All the kids except for Horace Splattly, who was too busy drawing a picture of himself as the Cupcaked Crusader to notice. Dienow's bright metal ruler spun through the air like a knife, slicing a spike of hair off Horace's head before stabbing the wall.

Horace watched as the clipped lock dropped from his head and fell across his nose. He frowned. He loved his short, spiky black hair and didn't like to see it cut by anyone but himself, especially not his mean science teacher. "Uh, Mr. Dienow," Horace asked, "do you think you could be more careful where you throw your ruler?"

Mr. Dienow chuckled. "I suppose I could try, but what would be the fun in that? Now, does anyone have an answer for me?"

Dienow picked the bone off his desk and slapped it across his palm. He walked between the students' desks and stopped by Horace's, sticking the tip of the bone in Horace's nostril. "Do you know what this is?" he said.

Horace gazed up at his teacher. Dienow loved picking on him because he was the smallest kid in Blootinville Elementary except for the kindergartners and six of the first graders. Horace sniffed. The bone smelled like a rotten egg. Or maybe *Dienow* smelled like a rotten egg. Horace wasn't sure. He held his breath and answered his teacher's question. "Uh, sorry, sir. I don't know what bone that is, sir."

Mr. Dienow pulled the bone out of Horace's nose and smiled. "All right then, we'll do something else to finish our last class. Mr. Splattly, do you have any subjects you'd like us to talk about?"

Horace leaned forward on his desk. "I sure do, sir. Uh, how about we talk about all the aliens who come down to Earth and try to take us back to their planets," he said.

Kids laughed.

Mr. Dienow's eyes grew red and shiny, and he struck the bone against Horace's desk, making

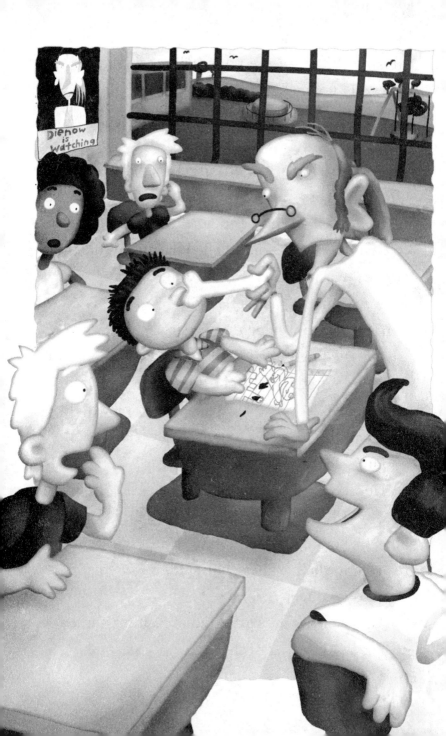

Horace jump in his seat. "I have a much better idea," he said. "Remember the first day of science class in September when we all measured ourselves? Since then, I think most of you have grown three, four, or even *five* inches." He grabbed the back of Horace's head and gave it a shake. "On the other hand, I don't think Horace Splattly has grown one inch all school year. Why don't we measure him and find out." The teacher lifted Horace from his seat so Horace's feet dangled in the air.

Horace groaned. He was only two feet and six inches tall. Kids were always teasing him about being so little.

But Mr. Dienow was the only teacher who did.

Horace looked desperately across the room to his two best friends, the Blootin twins.

Auggie (rhymes with "froggy") saw that his friend was in trouble. He combed his long blond bangs across the top of his head and spoke. "Uh, Mr. Dienow, I don't think that would be fun. Maybe we should talk about that bone some more, huh?"

Xax (rhymes with "tacks") nodded. He shook his long blond bangs over his eyes and spoke. "Uh, that bone sure looks mighty bony. . . . I'd s-sure hate to go on vacation without knowing more about it."

Dienow ignored the boys. He walked Horace to the front of the room, set him on the desk, and picked up a measuring tape. "Now, let's see if Horace has grown since our first science class, shall we?"

Back in September, Dienow had told everyone that he'd seen Horace at the Celernip Festival that summer, sitting on his mother's lap on the merry-go-round because he was too short to ride a horse alone.

Now it was a whole school year later. Mr. Dienow flipped his class book open and thumbed through the pages. "According to my notes, Horace Splattly was only two feet and six inches tall at the start of this school year."

Cyrus Splinter spoke up. He was the tallest kid in Blootinville Elementary by a foot and a half and the meanest by five and one-quarter Blootometers. "Are you sure he's that big?" Cyrus asked. "He looks about the size of a Tater Tot."

The whole class laughed except for Auggie, Xax, and Horace.

Mr. Dienow pulled on his chin. "All right then, how many people think Horace has grown? Raise your hands."

Only Auggie, Xax, and Horace raised their hands.

"I think he looks even shorter than he did in September," Cyrus joked.

Kids laughed again.

"Wouldn't it be interesting if Horace has shrunk?" Dienow said.

Horace looked across the room at Sara Willow. He thought she was the most beautiful girl he'd ever seen, and he was always hoping she'd notice him. And now she was smiling right at him. Of course, Horace wasn't sure if she was smiling at him because she liked him or because she thought he looked funny. . . .

Dienow held the end of the measuring tape to the tip of Horace's feet and stretched it to the top of his head. He pressed his palm down against Horace's spiky hair so it wouldn't get measured as part of his height.

"How much taller am I?" Horace asked. "I must be a couple inches taller."

Dienow released the end of the measuring tape, and it spooled into the reel with a loud snap. "Two feet six inches exactly!" the teacher shouted with glee. "Horace Splattly hasn't grown one inch! He'll *still* have to ride the merry-go-round while sitting on his mommy's lap!"

All the kids laughed again except for Auggie, Xax, and Horace.

Auggie dropped his head into his hands and shook it back and forth.

Xax looked at the floor and started counting all the scuff marks.

Horace just stared out at the class, his face turning red. Everyone was laughing at him because he was so little. Even Sara Willow. In fact, *she* was laughing so hard, her mouth was open wide enough to fit around the opening of a peanut-butter jar. If they knew he was the Cupcaked Crusader, Horace thought, they wouldn't be laughing. Then they wouldn't care that he was little. Then Sara Willow would want to be his girlfriend.

The school bell rang. Kids leaped from their seats, grabbed their backpacks from under their desks, and raced to the door.

"Halt, vile beasts!" Dienow yelled. "Where do you think you're going?"

The kids moaned.

"What kind of bone is this?" their teacher demanded.

No one had an answer. Horace remained standing on the teacher's desk. He was too little to get down without Dienow's help.

"All right—all right!" Dienow yelled. "I can't believe you're all too stupid to recognize the leg bone of our beloved town mascot: the wild pink dodo!" The teacher slammed the bone against the blackboard, splintering it into thousands of tiny pieces. "Get out of here!" he bellowed at the top of his voice. "Get out of my classroom, you idiots!"

Kids ran from the room as fast as carrots running from a very hungry rabbit (if carrots had legs to run away from rabbits).

Dienow scooped Horace off his desk and dropped him to the floor like a piece of trash. "See you at the Celernip Festival in two weeks," he said with a nasty smile. "Have a fun ride on the merry-go-round."

Horace grabbed his backpack and walked from the classroom without a word. There had to be *something* he could do so everyone would stop making fun of him for being short.

THE CELERNIP PRINCE

"All boys ten to fourteen years old, please take a flyer," Principal Nosair called as the kids ran to their buses, bikes, motorized skateboards, and hang gliders. The principal stuffed the pale green paper into Horace's hand. "Start getting ready. The pageant's only two weeks away."

Horace walked down the school steps, still frowning about how everyone had laughed at him. Just because he was little, kids thought they could pick on him. It wasn't fair! He had to do something so everyone would stop it. He stood by Auggie and Xax. The three boys dropped their backpacks to the ground and read the papers in their hands:

This was the first year Horace and his friends were old enough to enter the Celernip Prince Pageant. But he wasn't sure if he should. He didn't really care about it and never had. He knew his eight-year-old sister, Melody, would want him to enter. Ever since she was four and dressed Horace up in doll clothes, she'd wanted her brother to be old enough to be in the pageant. Now he was. And because Melody was taller and bigger and smarter than he was, she'd probably try to force him to be in it.

"Are you guys going to enter?" Horace asked his best friends. "I don't think I want to, but Melody will probably make me."

"You think so?" Auggie asked, stuffing his flyer in his backpack. "Do you think she'd make you eat some of her superpower cupcakes so you'd win?"

"I'd never let her do that," Horace said. "That wouldn't be fair."

Auggie wrinkled his brow with worry. "But what if your sister made you eat them? Then you'd have powers and you could easily beat everyone. And you know your sister always does mean stuff to you to get what she wants."

Horace nodded. "That's true," he said.

Xax looked up from his flyer. "Did you know there are three hundred eighty-two letters, numbers, and punctuation marks on the pageant announcement?" he asked.

Auggie took the paper from his brother, rolled it into a tube, and batted Xax on the head. "Why do you always count so much?"

Xax shrugged. "I like to. Isn't that a good reason?"

"So, are you guys entering the pageant?" Horace asked again.

"Definitely," Xax said. "We've both wanted to be Celernip Prince forever. Our mom and dad said that one of us should win this year and then the other next year."

Cyrus Splinter pushed his way between the boys. "You losers don't have a chance," he said, pointing at the twins. "Your dad may be mayor, but my great-great-great-great-grandfather is the person who crossed a turnip with a stalk of celery to invent the celernip! If it weren't for my family, there wouldn't be a Celernip Festival! All the judges know that, so I'm sure they'll want me to win." He looked at Horace. "And you're so little, if you stood onstage, the audience would think you were a smudge of dirt. Janitor Soilly would probably rush onstage and mop you away."

Horace tilted his chin up at Cyrus. "I'd be bigger than a smudge," he argued. "I'd be at least the size of a *pile* of dirt."

Cyrus laughed. "A dancing, singing pile of dirt." He sneered and walked off across the school yard.

"That's the last straw!" Horace said, stomping a foot to the ground and raising a puff of dust. "That big clod-o-saurus! Maybe I wasn't going to enter before, but now I will. I'll show him and Dienow and *everyone* that just because I'm little doesn't mean I can't be the best! I'm not going to be a smudge of dirt! I'm going to be Celernip Prince and—"

"Oh, I can't wait!" a girl shrieked. "I just can't wait!"

That sweet, familiar voice caused Horace to look away from the twins and across the school yard. Sara Willow stood chatting with her friends. Her beautiful hair gleamed in the sunlight. She wore it in a different style every day. Today it was decorated to look like a windmill.

"Now that I'm ten, I'm getting a fancy dress to go to the Celernip Ball," Sara said. "I'm having my hair cut by Madame Chantilly Bellray. She's making a special style just for me."

Horace jumped up and down and shook each twin by the shoulders. "That's perfect!" he said. "I'll win the Celernip Prince Pageant and then

Sara will like me! She can be my Celernip Princess and we'll be the most popular kids in all of Blootinville! We'll be on TV and in parades and then we'll always be on the same dodgeball team in gym! We'll call each other on the phone every night and talk about what we're going to wear at school the next day so we always, always match. I'm sure she'll also want to come over to my house after school every day so we can do homework while sipping celernip sodas. She'd probably even get her hair done in the shape of my head and have my name tattooed on her forehead in big letters. And once she does that, I'll know for sure that she really, really likes me forever, so I could tell her I'm the Cupcaked Crusader and she'd be able to keep the secret! And once she knows that, I could tell her to be your friend, too. Then we could all work together to solve all the mysteries in our *Splattly and Blootin Big Notebook of Worldwide Conspiracies!*" Horace smiled at his friends. "What do you think of that plan? Pretty great, huh?"

Auggie and Xax dropped their mouths open.

Horace continued. "We could even call it *The Willow, Splattly, and Blootin Big Notebook of Worldwide Conspiracies!*"

Auggie leaned into Horace's face. "Are you completely nuts? You can't tell her anything! She's one of the popular kids who doesn't even like us."

"She'll like me when I'm Celernip Prince," Horace answered.

"Why does she get her name on the notebook in front of ours?" Xax asked.

Auggie took Horace's arm and stared his friend hard in the eyes. "We're *never* going to tell her about the notebook. Right?"

Xax took Horace's other arm. "You, me, and Auggie started writing that book when we were in first grade. Those are *our* secrets."

Horace wriggled away from the twins. "I'll tell her when I'm Celernip Prince," he said. "Then it will be okay."

Xax shook his bangs over his eyes. "Not without our permission. And we said no!"

"You're going to ruin everything just because

you're mad at Dienow and Cyrus. And Sara will just think you're dumb anyway," Auggie said.

"Why can't you just be the Cupcaked Crusader?" Xax said. "Can't you let one of us be Celernip Prince? You didn't even want to be until Cyrus picked on you."

Horace walked a circle around his friends. "But the more I think about it, the more it makes sense. If I got to be Celernip Prince and made Sara my Celernip Princess, then everyone would stop making fun of me because they'd think that if she liked me, then I must be a great guy! And once I'm Celernip Prince, everyone will be interested in what I have to say, so I could start making speeches about all the stuff in our notebook. I could even tell everyone about how we think a giant five-eyed bee lives underwater in Lake Honkaninny and is going to come out and sting everyone."

"We don't *want* to tell everyone about that stuff," Auggie said.

"Those are just stories for us to figure out," Xax said.

Auggie picked his backpack off the ground and slung it over his shoulder. "You just want more attention," he said. "You think that just because you're little and are the Cupcaked Crusader, Xax and I should let you do things your way all the time. Well, that's not going to happen. And since we have the notebook at our house, we're not going to let you see it until you grow your brain back and give up stupid ideas about sharing it with your Celernip Princess. Come on, Xax, let's go home and start preparing for the pageant."

Xax picked up his backpack and the two brothers walked toward the parking lot, where their limousine waited.

"Hey, wait!" Horace called. "I don't need all the attention. I'm just doing it so no one makes fun of me."

Auggie and Xax ignored him and kept walking.

Horace picked up his backpack and was about to run after them when he heard a shout.

"Look up at those beautiful balloons!" a kid called.

"Where did they come from?" a girl asked.

Horace and all the other kids in the school yard looked up. High above their heads, two balloons floated. Each balloon was in the shape of the Cupcaked Crusader riding on the back of a pink dodo bird. Long pink ribbons dangled down from the balloons. All the kids cheered and reached for the ribbons.

"It's for the Celernip Festival!" Sara Willow cried. "I bet whoever catches them will win special prizes!"

Horace stared, confused. Why would someone make balloons of the Cupcaked Crusader riding a dodo? Was he really that popular? He watched as kids began screaming and running after the balloons. Some climbed jungle gyms, some shimmied up trees, and others flapped their arms, hoping to fly.

Sara did two ballerina twirls, a leap, and gave her windmill hairdo a spin. She lifted off the ground for long enough to grab hold of the long pink ribbon attached to one of the balloons. "It's mine! I've got one!" she cried.

Auggie and Xax chased after the other one. Auggie climbed atop his brother's shoulders. "Get on your tiptoes," he ordered. "Lean this way! No, back a bit! No, this way again." He stretched his arm as high as he could and grabbed the ribbon. "I've got it!" he yelled. "It's ours!"

But just as Sara tied the ribbon to her wrist and Auggie tied the ribbon to his belt and held on to his brother's head to keep his balance, the two balloons lifted all three children off the ground and into the air.

UP, UP, UP. THEN DOWN, DOWN, DOWN.

Principal Nosair and all the kids in the school yard looked up at the sky, where Sara Willow and the Blootin twins floated high above their heads.

"Someone help me!" Sara yelled.

"Get us down!" Auggie shouted. His legs were wrapped around Xax's neck, and Xax held tight to them so he wouldn't fall.

Principal Nosair surveyed the situation. "Those balloons fly better than real dodos," he said. "I must alert the Blootinville International Airport and Garbage Dump so they can send a

rescue team." He took out his cell phone and dialed.

"What if the balloons explode before they get to them?" one kid asked.

Horace knew he had to act fast. He stuffed the Celernip Festival announcement in his pocket and raced behind a bush. From inside his backpack, he took out a purple taffeta suit and a small aluminum ball containing one special afterschool treat.

The Cupcaked Crusader would save all three of them.

Horace slipped his costume over his clothes and unwrapped the ball of foil. It contained a new type of cupcake his sister had baked last week. It had a green cake bottom and top with a layer of horseradish frosting in the middle. His sister didn't usually give him cupcakes for the fun of it, so Horace had had to beg her for one and promise to wash and iron her Lily Deaver Scout uniforms every afternoon for a month.

Horace shoved the piece of cake in his mouth and began chewing.

Immediately, he felt as if something had gone terribly, terribly wrong. Melody's superpower-giving cupcakes had never made him feel as weird as this before.

• • •

Melody was the mastermind behind the cup-cakes. Horace's sister was an eight-year-old mad-scientist–baker–genius–Lily Deaver Scout. She made the cupcakes so Horace would have superpowers to fly, breathe fire, and do other amazing stuff. But because Melody only wanted

Horace to have powers when *she* wanted him to do stuff, like spy on kids she didn't like, she made the cupcakes so the powers wouldn't last for very long.

Melody also sewed Horace his Cupcaked Crusader costume so no one would know who he was. She was afraid that if their mom and dad found out she was baking such dangerous cupcakes and making Horace eat them, they'd take away her lavender Lily Deaver Spill & Brew Science Laboratory, her lavender Lily Deaver Cook & Bake Oven, and her lavender Lily Deaver lab coat, rubber gloves, and measuring spoons with the built-in digital cameras.

She forced Horace to wear the Cupcaked Crusader costume whenever he ate the cupcakes and got superpowers. Auggie and Xax were the only two people besides Melody who knew Horace was the Cupcaked Crusader. And she'd be really angry if she found out he'd told them.

And even though he didn't like the purple outfit or being called the Cupcaked Crusader,

Horace did like being a superhero so he could save people. After all, he thought, it was better to be a purple superhero than not to be a superhero at all.

• • •

Horace stood on the playground in the purple taffeta Cupcaked Crusader outfit. The costume covered him from toe to fingertip. It had a cape, wings, and a large stiff collar. It also had a hood Horace pulled over his face so no one would recognize him. The thick cloth of his cape rustled in the warm June breeze.

Horace finished chewing the green cupcake with the layer of horseradish icing in the middle. It tasted bitter and gross like it had been soaked in vinegar, cough medicine, and paste. But what was even weirder was that it was icy cold. Goose bumps broke out across Horace's entire body. He began shivering and his teeth chattered even though it was over eighty degrees outside. And then the sickest thing happened.

Inside his mouth, each of the pieces of the cupcake grew tiny legs and crawled around like insects. Horace stuck out his tongue and tried to spit them out, but when he opened his mouth, the cupcake beetles formed two lines and crawled past his lips and up his nostrils.

Horace clutched his head. He felt like he had creepy-crawly ice cubes under the skin on his face. He grabbed at his cheeks, rubbed his forehead, and pinched the skin between his eyes, hoping to make the beetles go away. The cold hurt so much, he shut his eyes and waited. After about fifteen more seconds, the crawly cake beetles seemed to have disappeared. The only thing that felt strange was a cold tingling behind his eyes.

Horace blinked. Immediately, two ten-foot-long ice rays shot out of his eyes and exploded in the sky above his head.

"What was that?" a kid asked.

"Where did that ice explosion come from?"

Horace ran from behind the bush into the crowd of kids in the school yard.

"The Cupcaked Crusader's here to save every-one!" a kid cheered.

"Hurry and help them, Cupcaked Crusader!"

Horace looked up at Sara and the twins. A flock of vultures was circling the kids, eyeing them hungrily. Xax's hands shook with pain from holding on to his brother's legs so tight. How could Horace save them? The only power he had was to blink and shoot ice beams into the air.

"You must do something, Cupcaked Crusader," Principal Nosair called.

Who to save first? The Blootins? Sara? How could he decide? What should he do?

Horace turned his eyes to the sky and saw a vulture diving straight at Sara.

"HELP ME!" she screamed.

There was only one thing the Cupcaked Crusader could think to do. Horace blinked, and two ice beams shot fifty feet in the air, striking the dodo balloon. The balloon exploded, and something sparkly and pink dropped out of it and attached itself to Sara Willow's head. A second later, she was falling from the sky.

Kids screamed. "She'll hit the ground!" a boy yelled.

"Why did you pop the balloon, Cupcaked Crusader?" a girl cried.

"She'll break all her bones!" a boy shouted.

Horace had wanted to keep Sara from floating away and being attacked by the vultures, but had completely forgotten about how he'd get her to the ground. Sara's hair windmill spun faster and faster as she fell. What could a superhero with super-icicle powers do to save a damsel in distress?

If Horace didn't come up with an answer fast, Sara Willow would have a lot more problems than just a messy windmill hairdo.

THE SHINIEST SCALPS
HORACE HAD EVER SEEN

Horace got into his favorite thinking pose. He put the forefinger of his left hand on his chin and the forefinger of his right hand in his ear and twisted it in a circle. And just like that— he got an idea! Quickly, Horace blinked four times, each time aiming his eyes higher and higher. Ice beams shot out over and over and over until Horace had built an ice slide that stretched high into the sky. Sara Willow fell right onto it, landing at the top, then sliding down to the school yard.

All the kids cheered.

"The Cupcaked Crusader saved Sara Willow!"

"Hooray for the Cupcaked Crusader!"

"Isn't this the third time he's had to save her?" one kid asked.

"Hey! What about us, Cupcaked Crusader?" Xax shouted.

"Yeah," Auggie yelled. "Just because we're not as pretty as Sara doesn't mean we shouldn't be saved too, huh?" The vultures dove closer and closer to the twins. One of the birds even took a peck at Xax's foot, eating off the front of his sneaker.

"Yikes! He almost got my big toe!" Xax screamed.

Horace looked up, blinked his eyes, and shot ice beams at the second dodo balloon. The balloon popped, and a sparkly pink thing fell out and attached itself to Auggie's head. As the twins tumbled through the air, Horace blinked four more times, making another ice slide. The two boys dropped right into it and slid safely to the ground.

All the kids cheered for the Cupcaked Crusader.

Sara Willow and the twins stood quietly, obviously still in shock. Horace observed Auggie and Sara up close. He could see that what had fallen out of the balloons and stuck to their heads were sparkly pink butterfly hair clips. Auggie tried to pick his out, but it wouldn't come loose.

"Help me with this, Xax," he said.

Xax tugged on it.

"Don't pull so hard!" Auggie said.

"You said to get it out!" Xax said.

Horace stepped toward Sara. "Are you okay, miss? I hope you're not hurt."

Sara began crying. "It was so scary," she wept. "And my windmill's a mess! This clip got stuck in it and—"

Horace gave her arm a gentle pat. "Don't worry, lovely lady, we'll get it out. It's just a butterfly hair clip. It actually looks quite pretty."

"It's not pretty when it's in a boy's hair," Cyrus joked. "I think we should call Auggie Augustina."

"No way!" Auggie said, pulling even harder at the hair clip.

"I don't care how pretty it is," Sara said. "Today I'm celebrating windmills, not butter-flies!" She reached a hand up and tried to yank the clip from her hair.

Suddenly both butterfly clips began flapping across Auggie's and Sara's heads.

"AYAAEEEEE!" Sara yelled. "What's happen-ing?!"

"Something's not feeling good up there!" Auggie said. "Make it stop!"

Before anyone could make a move, the clips rapidly snapped across both kids' heads, as if the clips were mouths with real teeth instead of plastic ones. They snapped over and over until all the hair was gone, then stopped. Auggie and Sara now stood on the playground totally bald except for the hair clips stuck to the tops of their heads. Their scalps were so smooth and shiny, it hurt to look at them in the direct sunlight.

Sara felt her bald scalp and the hair clip.

"H-how could this happen?!" she screamed at the top of her lungs. She looked at the Cupcaked Crusader. "Why did you pop the balloon and make this clip land on me? I'd rather have flown away! Now I can't go to the Celernip Ball!" She lifted her skirt over her head and ran off the school grounds.

Auggie tugged on the clip, but it wouldn't come loose from his scalp.

Horace looked at his friend. "Uh, sorry about that thing eating your hair," he said, still using his Cupcaked Crusader voice so other kids wouldn't know who he was.

Auggie stared angrily at Horace, took his arm, and dragged him away from the crowd of kids. "How am I going to be Celernip Prince with a butterfly hair clip on my head?" he whispered in Horace's ear. "Did you and Melody plan this so it would be easier for you to win?"

"What are you talking about?" Horace asked. "I saved you!"

"Then why was the balloon shaped like you riding a dodo? And why weren't you chasing after the balloons trying to catch them like everyone else?" Auggie asked.

Horace gasped. "I was just surprised to see the balloons," he said. "You know I could never do anything so mean. I'm not even smart enough to make anything so crazy."

"Maybe *you're* not," Auggie said, looking around the playground. "But I don't see *Melody* around anywhere. And she's smart enough to make those balloons. *And* you admitted that she'd do *anything* to have you win. Maybe you knew about this *before* it happened."

"Are you saying that Melody and I planned this?" Horace asked. "That's nuts!"

Auggie put his hands on his hips and turned to his brother. "You know what? I think Melody and Horace really wanted the second balloon to eat off *your* hair, Xax. That's why Horace saved Sara first. It was only an accident that she caught that balloon. It was supposed to happen to *you*."

Xax gave Horace a mean look. "Wow, Horace, I didn't think you'd ever let your sister hurt us just so you could win the pageant. You were our best friend ever."

Auggie nodded. "Come on, Xax. I think this is something we need to write in *The Splattly and Blootin Big Notebook of Worldwide Conspiracies*." The twins walked across the yard and climbed into the back of the limousine.

Horace stomped his foot. "You can't put me in that book! That's a book for evil, scary stuff, and I'm—I'm a hero!" He stomped his foot again. "I didn't send those balloons up in the air!"

The limousine door slammed shut and the twins drove off home.

Principal Nosair walked over to the Cupcaked Crusader and gave him a pat on the head. "This was certainly an exciting last day of school," he said. "I'll make sure everyone knows you're a hero, even if you did make Sara Willow and Auggie Blootin bald." He clapped his hands. "Now everyone head home for the summer. Remember, there are only eighty-six days until school starts again in September. I'll be sending you e-mails all summer with tips on how to get ready for the next school year."

The kids groaned and took off for home. Principal Nosair walked back into the school.

Crea–plunk! The two ice slides collapsed to the ground in a pile of melting splinters.

Horace stepped behind some bushes and

slipped off his Cupcaked Crusader costume. He stood alone and frowned.

First everyone in science class had laughed at him for being so little, and *now* the twins were mad at him for being a show-off. They thought he was so mean that he and his sister would plan to hurt them to stop them from winning the Celernip Prince Pageant. And to top *that* off, Sara was mad at the Cupcaked Crusader because the butterfly hair clip had eaten her hair.

Horace thought this had to be the worst last day of school he'd ever had.

Chapter 5

FROM SHRIMP TO PRINCE?

"**H**ey there, Horace my boy, how was your last day of school?" Dr. Hinkle Splattly stood on the front lawn as Horace walked up the sidewalk. Horace's dad worked in an office that had a separate entrance from the house. He was a psychiatric doctor who helped people who had problems they needed to talk about. At the end of each fifty-minute appointment, Dr. Splattly stepped into the part of the house where the family lived and checked up on Horace and Melody. Horace's mom was the publisher of the *Blootinville Banner*, the town newspaper. She didn't get home until seven o'clock.

"It was okay," Horace answered.

Dr. Splattly held Horace's shoulders and gave his son a curious look. "Aren't you happy it's the last day of school?"

"I guess," Horace said.

"And isn't the Celernip Festival in two weeks? I hope you're going to compete to be Celernip Prince." Dr. Splattly smiled at Horace. "I'm sure your sister would love to help you."

"That's what I'm afraid of," Horace said.

Dr. Splattly laughed and walked over to his office entrance. "See you in an hour," he told his son.

Horace stepped into the house and ran up the stairs and into Melody's room. "What's going on?" he asked. "You didn't wait for me to walk home with you."

Melody sat at her desk wearing her lavender Lily Deaver sewing coat and sewing a colorful orange-and-pink shirt with her Lily Deaver Stitch & Sew machine. "Honestly, Horace, how many times do I have to wait after school while you show off as the Cupcaked Crusader to save some dumb little kid who gets into trouble? I really don't have the time for it."

Horace frowned, thought about Auggie and Xax, and dropped his backpack to the floor. "I'm not a show-off," he said.

"Hmm . . ." Melody replied. "All I know is that the minute something goes wrong, you instantly appear as the Cupcaked Crusader."

Horace glared at his sister. "So what did you have to rush home for? Just to do some sewing?" he asked. "Didn't you see what happened to Auggie and Sara?"

"Oh, Horace, do you think it really matters if a couple little kids go bald? Aren't there more important things in life to worry about?" Melody curled her lower lip over her top lip, then smiled, yanking the orange-and-pink fabric from her sewing machine and holding it before her brother. "Do you like it?" she asked. "What do you think?"

Horace ignored his sister and flopped down

on her bed, staring at the ceiling. "I don't care about that. Didn't you see what happened? Auggie and Xax think we sent those balloons up and made those clips that ate off Sara's and Auggie's hair."

Melody laughed. "They think we did that?"

"Yeah," Horace said, rolling over to see his sister's face. "Uh, you didn't *really* do it, did you?"

Melody hung the shirt over the back of her chair and walked over to her brother. "First of all, I wouldn't do anything mean to Auggie or Sara. Why would I? I have no reason to be afraid of them. And secondly, they'd have to be stupid to think I'd ever let you in on anything I was planning," Melody declared. "After all, I'm the one in charge here. You're just a tool I use to get what I want."

Horace sat up on the bed. "Fine, so you didn't do it, but they still *think* we did. Can you make me some cupcakes so I can find out who *really* did it and capture him?"

Melody reached over to her brother and

pulled the green slip of paper announcing the Celernip Prince Pageant from his jean pocket. "See this, shrimp?" she asked.

Horace scowled and looked down at the piece of paper. "Of course, that's about the pageant. I was going to enter it before all this happened, but now I have to find out who made those balloons. That's more important."

Melody unfolded the piece of paper and waved it in Horace's face. "It's been one of my lifelong dreams to know I could turn a talentless, little imp like you into the Celernip Prince of Blootinville. And now you're finally old enough to enter the pageant, so that's *exactly* what's going to happen. Understand?"

"I would like to win the pageant, but finding out who did this is more important, okay?" he told her. "Can't you understand that?"

Melody leaned over her brother and touched a finger to his nose, slowly pressing it back until Horace was lying flat on the bed. "I understand that, but I think making you the greatest

Celernip Prince this town has ever seen is more important. So unless you do what I say, I'll flush all my ingredients down the toilet and *never* make you another cupcake again. Which means you won't be able to figure out who sent up those balloons and Auggie and Xax will hate you for the rest of their lives. Can't *you* understand *that*?" Melody took the shirt she'd been sewing off the back of the chair.

Horace got off the bed. "I'll let you help me

win the pageant," he told her, thinking that maybe she would have some good ideas for him. "But can't you make me the cupcakes *first* so I can figure out who's doing this?"

Melody tossed the orange-and-pink shirt over Horace's head and laughed. "*I* make the decisions around here, not you. So try on your costume. Then we'll start practicing your celernip tap dance. When I'm ready to make the cupcakes, I will."

Horace looked down at the shirt. It had big ruffles around the cuffs and collar and was covered with pictures of orange celernips and pink dodos. He groaned and fell facedown on Melody's bed, pressing his nose into a pillow. If he ever wanted to be the Cupcaked Crusader again and solve the mystery of the balloons, it looked as if he'd first have to be his sister's living, breathing Celernip Prince doll.

THE SPLATTLY MASH & SPLAT

Six days had passed since the last day of school. Everyone in town had heard about the Cupcaked Crusader balloons that had exploded and made Auggie and Sara bald, but since the superhero had also saved Auggie and Sara from floating away, no one believed the Cupcaked Crusader had planned it . . . except for Auggie and Xax.

Horace still hadn't heard from his best friends. He'd phoned four times and left messages, but they never called him back.

In the meantime, Melody made Horace practice for the pageant.

She made her brother run laps around the

block carrying a suitcase full of celernips so he'd be in good shape in case she wanted him to wear a skimpy celernip bathing suit.

She made him wear a crown of celernips on his head until they were rotten and smelly to see how long he could sit still.

And today, Horace stood in the front yard, stomping inside a large steel bucket full of celernips.

Melody pushed a button on her CD player. The music to "Row, Row, Row Your Boat" filled the air, and she waved her lavender Lily Deaver baton. "Begin!" she ordered.

Horace hopped in the bucket and sang, "Smash, smash, smash your celernip; smash it so it's smooth; crush it, bash it, stomp it, blast it; so babies eat it with one tooth." He stopped. The smashed celernips stuck to his legs and oozed between his toes. "This is disgusting. You've turned me into a human blender. I want to win, but still, why can't you just make me some cupcakes now, and then I'll practice later?"

"Absolutely not. You'll appreciate the cup-

cakes more if you work for them." Melody
poked her brother in the nose with the baton.
"Stomp!" she commanded.

Horace gritted his teeth, reached into the
bucket, and scooped out a fistful of celernips.
He raised it at his sister. "You know, I don't have
to do everything you tell me to."

Melody swung her baton at her older brother's fist, splattering the celernip all over Horace's
face and clothes. "Oh, shrimpy, you're just so
funny when you get mad." She giggled. "And
you know that if you want the cupcakes, you
have to do what I tell you."

Horace swiped his hands across his face, clearing the celernip from his eyes. There was no point in arguing with his sister. Because she was right.

A whirring sound filled his ears, and he looked up to see a green-and-yellow-striped helicopter swoop over the Splattly home and settle in the middle of the street.

Everyone in town knew who owned the helicopter. It belonged to Penny Honey, the seven-year-old rich girl who lived in a four-story mansion with a gold mermaid fountain on the front lawn. She was always making Melody angry by showing off her fancy things and acting like she was the best at everything she did.

The helicopter's door swung open, and Penny leaped out doing a ballerina pirouette. She was wearing a twenty-four-karat-gold T-shirt and a platinum skirt. On the shirt, the phrase RHYMES WITH RICH was spelled out in diamonds. "Hiya, Melody," Penny purred. She did a few more leaps across the lawn and kicked up a foot so her toes pointed at Melody's nose. "Look at my new chinchilla-fur sneakers! Mommy and Daddy let me buy them because it was the last day of school!" she screamed with delight.

Melody frowned, then forced herself to smile. "Gee, Penny, they look pretty. But won't fur sneakers be warm in the summer?"

"Not for me. I *never* go anywhere that isn't air-conditioned."

Melody waved her baton impatiently. "So, uh, what's going on?"

Penny did a small leap in the air. "Well, I saw you and Horace practicing for the Celernip Prince Pageant, and I just thought you'd like to know who I've been coaching."

Melody scrunched her forehead. "Who could you be coaching? You don't have a brother," she said.

Penny twirled a lock of her curly blond hair. "True. But my mom's friend has a boy I've been helping." She curtsied, then waved a hand to the helicopter. "Presenting my star pupil."

There, doing a cartwheel out the door of the

chopper, was none other than Auggie Blootin!

Horace couldn't believe his eyes.

Auggie was dressed in a green-and-white leotard and had a pile of shredded celernips covering his scalp so you couldn't see that he was bald and had a butterfly clip stuck to his head. Auggie flipped and twisted and twirled while juggling three celernips. He did backward and forward handsprings while tossing the celernips in the air, catching them in his mouth, spitting them out, and balancing them on his nose. He twisted his body every which way and spelled out the letters C-E-L-E-R-N-I-P.

"Fantabu-loosicous job, Auggie," Penny said, clapping her hands. She waved to the helicopter. "All right, you can come out now, Xax. Auggie's done." She wrinkled her nose and leaned in to Melody and Horace. "I'm *not* coaching Xax. He's just too uncoordinated to win, so why bother?"

Xax stepped onto the lawn. "I'm making up my own song and dance," he said. "I don't need a coach."

Penny twirled a curl of her hair. "Of course you don't," she said, giving Melody, Auggie, and Horace a wink.

"Well, what do you think?" Auggie asked Horace. "Pretty good, huh?" He did a twirl in his celernip costume. "We were just visiting Penny, and now she's flying us home."

Penny did a twirl on her toes. "If Auggie wins, I'm going to be his Celernip Princess." She smiled at Melody. "Are you going to be your little brother's Celernip Princess?"

Melody looked to Horace. "Of course I am, right?"

Horace stared at his sister, bug-eyed. "Uh, I was going to ask Sara Willow to be my Celernip Princess," he replied.

Melody swatted Horace with her baton. "You're going to ask me!"

Horace shook his head. "I can't. The most important reason why I'm *trying* to be Celernip Prince is so I can make Sara Willow my Celernip Princess," he explained.

Melody grabbed her brother by the arm. "The most important reason you're doing this is because if you don't I'll push your head into that bucket of smashed celernips!"

Penny and Auggie began laughing loudly.

"Oh my!" Penny exclaimed. "You kids are too, too funny."

"I don't think you have to worry about Horace choosing Sara to be Celernip Princess," Auggie told Melody. "If all he can do is smash celernips, I don't think he'll be choosing anyone." Auggie looked to Horace with a hard, cold stare. "Guess even by cheating and sending up those balloons, you still won't win the pageant, huh?"

"Me and my sister didn't send up those balloons," Horace said, leaning in and whispering in Auggie and Xax's ears. "And she's going to make me cupcakes so I can catch who really did it. Then I'm going to win the pageant and show you who's the best Celernip Prince in town."

"Aha!" Auggie said in a whisper. "So now you're planning to try and win with superpower cupcakes!"

Xax stepped between Auggie and Horace. "You—you—you can't eat superpower cupcakes to win!" he exclaimed. "Super-*anything* must be against the rules!"

"I didn't say I'd eat superpower cupcakes to try and win," Horace replied. "I said—"

"You're lying," Auggie said. "You and your sister would do anything to win."

"That's what you said at school," Xax said. "You don't care if it's against the rules or not."

"What's against the rules?" Melody asked.

"*Nothing's* against the rules," Horace said, ending the conversation so his friends wouldn't let Melody know that they knew about the cupcakes. "Auggie and Xax are just afraid I'm going to win."

Penny linked arms with Auggie and walked him to the helicopter. "Don't worry about him. I know you'll win. I'm sure Horace will look cute as a button in his costume, but being little and cute won't win the pageant, will it?"

"Yeah, you're probably right," Auggie said.

Xax leaned into Horace's ear. "I just want you to know that Auggie and I have already written *one* page about you in the notebook because of the balloons. If you eat cupcakes to win the pageant, we're going to write five or six more pages, then change the title of the book to *The Blootin Big Notebook of Worldwide Conspiracies All About the Cupcaked Crusader*." He ran across the yard and hopped into the helicopter.

Horace waved his fists in the air. "You can't put me in that notebook! That's my notebook, and after I win the pageant and prove I'm the best, then I'm going to get it back and put you and Auggie in it as the two biggest losers ever!" He dug his hands into the bucket of celernips, raised them above his head, and threw them at the helicopter's windows.

Unfortunately, the helicopter's blades were spinning, and when the smashed celernips hit them, the glop was sent flying back at Horace, splattering his cheeks. The whirlybird flew out of sight.

Melody gave her brother a withering look, then turned on her lavender Lily Deaver heels and headed toward the front door of the house.

"Where are you going?" Horace asked. "We have to practice for the pageant. You have to help me win so we prove to Penny and the Blootins that we're the best."

Melody glared at her brother. "I'm going inside to make some cupcakes, bubblehead. There's no way I'm going to let Auggie win so Penny can become Celernip Princess. I'm going to have to make you the best cupcakes ever so you can win the pageant. Otherwise, you're sure to lose." She flung the front door open, tossed her hair back, and marched into the house.

Horace watched his sister. Should he be angry with her for thinking he was too much of a loser to win the pageant *without* superpower cupcakes? Should he be happy she was making him superpower cupcakes? Should he cheat and eat the cupcakes so he could win the pageant and show Auggie, Xax, and everyone else that he could be the best Celernip Prince ever?

Horace wasn't sure, but he followed his sister into the house without another word.

THE SHORTEST CHAPTER
IN THE BOOK

That night, Horace climbed up the tree outside Melody's window and watched every move his sister made through his Splattly & Blootin Binoculars for Investigating Worldwide Conspiracies.

Melody was working busily in her room with her Lily Deaver Kitchenware and Cook & Bake Oven. She blended cockroaches, cinnamon, and horsehair into bowls of batter. She chopped in frog tongues, hot peppers, and bendy straws. But time after time, she threw her mixtures into the trash. "No, not good enough!" she said. "Not powerful enough!" "Not special enough—too

ugly!" she said, throwing away a funny-looking green cupcake.

Finally, after Horace had spent over an hour watching from the tree, Melody stepped out of her room and went downstairs. He took that moment to quickly climb through her bedroom window, snatch the ugly green cupcake out of Melody's trash can, and run down the hall to his room. *He* didn't care how the cupcake looked. He only hoped it gave him some really cool powers so he could catch whoever had made Auggie and Sara bald. He didn't even care that when Melody threw the cupcake in her trash can, it got pencil shavings all over the top of it and had a piece of chewed lavender Lily Deaver gum stuck to its side. He just wrapped it in foil and hid it in his backpack under his Cupcaked Crusader costume.

Then he went downstairs like any other ordinary kid in Blootinville and watched his favorite TV show, called *What's Up Your Nose?*

THE SECOND-SHORTEST CHAPTER IN THE BOOK

The next day, Horace woke to find Melody standing over his bed with her lavender Lily Deaver combination stopwatch and squirt gun in one hand. "Did you really think you were going to get away with this?" she asked. "Do you think I'm stupid?"

Did she know he'd taken the cupcake? Did she check her trash can? Horace sat up and rubbed his eyes. "Uh, I, uh, what are you talking about?" he asked.

Melody yanked Horace's arm, pulling him from the bed and onto the floor. "You can't win the contest by lying in bed all day. Get up. It's already six-fifteen. You should have begun practicing forty-five minutes ago."

Horace took a deep breath. She didn't know! The cupcake was safe. He yawned and curled into a ball, hugging his knees to his chest.

Melody nudged him with the toes of her lavender Lily Deaver construction boots. "Up, up, up!" she urged. "Time to get in some rehearsal time!"

Horace shut his eyes. Was being a superhero worth his sister ordering him around? Did *every* superhero have a younger sister who was bossy and mean? He tried to think of a way to get out of it. "Uh, but I thought you said I wasn't talented enough to win without superpowers, so you said you were going to bake me cupcakes. If that's true, then why do I have to practice?"

Melody leaned over her brother. "Horace, just because I'm making you cupcakes doesn't mean you can do nothing. You still need to *look* like you should be Celernip Prince. So get moving. I need to train you to walk like a prince, talk like a prince, bow like a prince, and do a jig like a prince." She clicked her stopwatch. "Okey-doke? So you have exactly five minutes to get outside and jog twenty-eight miles. Then come home so you can try on your costume and I can attach some more decorations. How does that sound?"

Horace sat up on the floor. "Uh, do you think I could bike instead of run?" he asked. "I like biking better."

Melody turned and walked toward the door. "Fine. Go bike up Rumbly Mountain. I'll pack you a celernip lunch. But make sure you're back by two P.M., got it?"

Horace looked at his backpack in the corner of the room. Time away from his sister meant time to investigate who had made Auggie and Sara bald. "Got it," he replied, leaping to his feet. "I'll just pack my backpack and be on my way."

Chapter 9

GETTING WIGGY

Horace pedaled along his street, Hip Hop Toad, turning his head to take in the view of the town.

He could see the tallest office tower at the town center where his mother worked as the publisher of the *Blootinville Banner*.

He could see the Chef Nibbles Canned Food Factory, which had closed earlier that year after Chef Nibbles had gotten himself into a heap of trouble with the Cupcaked Crusader.

He could see the Blootinville International Airport and Dump off to the south and the Nip and Tuck Plastic Surgery Center off to the west. He could even see as far as Derelict Cave and Society Hill, where the Blootins lived in their mansion, and Rumbly Mountain, where his sister thought he was going to exercise.

But Horace wasn't going to Rumbly Mountain. He knew exactly what had to be done. First, he would discover who sent up the balloons and catch him so Auggie and Xax would be his friends again. Second, he'd make up his own costume and routine to prove that he could win the pageant without his sister's help or superpower cupcakes. And third, once he won the pageant, he'd make Sara Willow his Celernip Princess and everyone would think Horace Splattly was the greatest kid in all of Blootinville.

At least Horace hoped it would work out that way.

He took his feet off the pedals, made a turn, and coasted along Main Street. Now, where was the best place to find someone who knew about bald people and butterfly hair clips?

Horace saw what he was looking for. He came to a stop and flipped down his kickstand. On the left side of the street was Madame

Chantilly Bellray's House of Beauty. On the right side of the street was Miss Kitty Hello's Hair Salon.

This looked like a good place to start.

The store windows of Miss Kitty Hello's Hair Salon were dusty. The red brick on the building was chipped and crumbly. When Horace took a second look at the sign above the door, he could see that the K in KITTY had been crossed out and been replaced with a pink B, and the words HAIR SALON had been crossed out and been replaced with the words WIG SHOP.

Horace wiped his hand across the dirty glass and peered inside Miss Bitty Hello's Wig Shop. There were piles and piles of hair covering the floor. Large cobwebs hung from wall to wall and ceiling to floor where hundreds of spiders made their homes.

Grrrrnnll-snnnrrrrrt.

Horace heard an odd noise and wiped more of the dirt from the window. There, sitting inside on the windowsill, lay a pig that was almost as big as Horace. The pig wore a long green wig and had a steel collar around his neck with the name WIGGLES spelled out in black letters.

Then Horace looked up and saw an even odder sight. In the center of the salon stood a tall woman wearing a gas mask and long black rubber dress. The woman held a can of hair spray in one hand and a blowtorch in the other. Spiders crawled up the woman's arms, around her neck, and down her back. But the woman didn't seem to care. She was too busy attending to a girl who sat wearing a hood over her head, but with very strange hair poking through the top. The only way Horace knew the girl in the chair was a girl was from her dress and pink shoes, which had the letter S on one foot and W on the other. The girl sat very still in the old dusty barber chair. The woman held the blow-torch and lit it so a small blue flame shot out of it. She aimed it at the girl's hair.

Horace looked from Miss Bitty Hello's Wig Shop across the street to Madame Chantilly Bellray's House of Beauty. Chantilly Bellray's shop was painted pink, and the inside was decorated with large statues of angels riding unicorns and unicorns riding angels. Women, men, girls, and boys streamed in and out of the entrance with bright smiling faces. The women and girls all had pretty hairdos tied with bows or fixed with headbands. The men and boys had neatly trimmed hair slicked back over their heads. Inside the salon, about fifteen people waited to get their hair done. Six hairdressers were busy at work cutting hair while Madame Chantilly Bellray danced around the salon in a white lace dress. She held a pair of golden scissors decorated with diamonds, pearls, rubies, and emeralds and pointed them at the customers' heads like a baton, conducting her haircutters, shampoo boys, and floor-sweeping girls.

Horace looked back to Miss Bitty Hello's Wig Shop, then stepped over to the door and pushed it open. The pig looked up, snorted at Horace, then went back to sleep. The woman working on the girl's hair stopped everything she was doing and peeled off her gas mask. Her face was as pink as frosting on a birthday cake, and her hair

was one large bright green wave that swooped up on one side of her head, then crashed down over the other. Small plastic dinosaurs stood on her head in a long line.

"Hello, I'm Bitty Hello. Do you need a wig?" she asked in a raspy voice, pointing her blow-torch at Horace. "Go sit in the corner. I'll be with you in a few minutes." The woman turned to the girl and rapped her knuckles against the girl's hair.

Bling. The girl's hair rang like a bell, and it looked like it was made from some kind of very thin metal.

Horace stepped toward Bitty. "Maybe I should just—"

"*Sit!*" Bitty commanded.

Horace backed away to a chair in the corner of the room. One of the four legs on the chair was broken. Horace had to balance on it very carefully so he wouldn't fall off into the big pile of dusty hair and crawling black spiders. As he wobbled on the chair, he noticed a photo on the wall of a woman who looked exactly like Bitty Hello except she was bald and had hair painted on her head. She also had a tattoo of a pig on her neck. Horace looked at Bitty as she took her blowtorch and burned holes through the metal wig on the girl's head. There was no pig tattoo on her neck, and she was obviously wearing a wig.

After a few minutes of painting and burning, Bitty stopped and peeled the hood off the girl's head. "Now don't you worry a bit, my dear," she said. "Soon all the boys and girls will want wigs just like yours." The girl's wig was a shiny, glimmering, smooth silver that flowed down to her shoulders in the back and to her chin in the front. When the girl turned and looked at Horace, all he could see of her were her two brown eyes staring out of the two holes that Bitty had cut for her.

The wig maker reached for the girl's wig. "Should I put it in a box or do you want to wear it home?" she asked.

The girl grabbed at the wig to keep it on her

head and stood. "I'll wear it home, thank you very much," she said. The girl handed the woman three one-hundred-dollar bills.

"Thank you so much, Miss Willow," Bitty said with a big smile. "Come back next week and I'll make you another. A bald girl can never have too many wigs."

The girl muttered a good-bye and dashed from the salon.

Horace's mouth dropped open. *Willow?* And *S.W.* on the shoes? *Sara Willow* was the girl who had just bought the wig! He watched as the love of his life hopped into the backseat of a car and drove away.

Spfft. The blowtorch blew past Horace's ear. "Well, sweetie, what can I do for you?" Bitty asked. "Looking to get a wig for the Celernip Ball?"

Horace gulped. "I—I just came to see, uh, if . . ." He didn't know what to say, and before he could get an answer out, Bitty lifted him by his armpits, hoisted him in the air, and plunked him down in the barber chair in front of a cracked, dusty mirror.

Chapter 10

BITTY & KITTY

Horace gazed at himself in the mirror. The crack ran down his forehead, across his nose, and through his lips. "I—I don't think I need a wig," he said. He rubbed a hand at his hair. "See? I have all my hair. It's very stuck to my head so—"

Spffft. Bitty lit the blowtorch and let out a loud laugh. "I can take care of that." She leaned in close to Horace, aiming the bright blue flame at his hair.

"*No!*" Horace cried. He leaped from the chair and raced across the room.

Bitty frowned, shut off the blowtorch, and slumped in the barber chair. "Well, if you're not here for a wig, what did you come in for?" she asked. She dropped the torch into a pile of hair on the floor. "You know, if more people in town don't go bald soon, I don't know what I'll do."

"Did a boy named Auggie Blootin come in for a wig?" Horace asked.

"No, that bald boy hasn't come in yet," Bitty said. "The little girl who was just here told me that he doesn't care about wearing a wig."

Horace walked over to the woman. "Why don't you cut hair so you'd get more business?" he asked.

The wig maker shook her head, and her wig slipped onto her lap, revealing her shiny, bald head. "Oh, I can't cut hair. I'm just terrible at it. I make wigs from steel, plastic, cardboard, or whatever else I find at the dump. If you're bald, you can have a different hairstyle every day. In fact, if people shaved their heads like I do, then tried my wigs, I bet they'd really like them." She pointed at the wig in her lap. "This is made out of the insulation from a broken refrigerator and plastic dinosaurs I got at a toy store."

"Is that in the photo on the wall?" Horace asked.

"Oh no—no," Bitty replied with a shake of her head. "That's my twin sister, Kitty. She used to run this salon, but then about a year ago, Chantilly Bellray came to town and took all her business away. Kitty was so upset, she left town and said she'd never come back. I just moved to Blootinville a few weeks ago, took over the shop, and started making wigs. But I guess not too many people here need wigs right now, huh?"

Wiggles lifted his head and grunted.

The clock in the town square struck eleven. "Well, if you don't need a wig, scram, kid," Bitty said, picking her wig off her lap. "I have to glue mine back on." She stepped through a door at the back of the room.

Horace looked around the salon. It was so dusty and shabby, he thought no one would ever come there for a wig unless they really, really needed one like Sara must have thought she did.

Loud shouts of excitement came from the street. Horace ran to the store window in time to see a crowd of people rushing out of Madame Chantilly Bellray's House of Beauty and all the other shops along Main Street. Over one hundred people stared at a humongous balloon of the Cupcaked Crusader riding a puffy pink dodo bird. The balloon was the size of a school bus.

"That's the prettiest bird balloon I ever saw," a woman said. "It must be in celebration of our Celernip Festival next week."

"I want to attach one to the roof of my house," a man said.

"Can I get one, Daddy?" a little girl asked.

"Maybe for your birthday," her dad answered.

Horace dashed out of Miss Bitty Hello's Wig Shop, hid behind a Dumpster, and dropped his backpack to the ground. He took out his Cupcaked Crusader costume and pulled it on over his clothes. Then he reached into his bag and pulled out the ball of foil with the cupcake from his sister's trash can.

He brushed off the pencil shavings and wad of gum, then examined the cupcake. It was an ugly green color, had chunks of celernip sticking out of the top, and a slimy black celernip root poking out of the bottom. A thin coat of blue fuzz was stuck to its side.

Horace looked up at the giant balloon and knew he'd better eat the cupcake right away. He put the fuzzy blue cupcake into his mouth and began chewing, biting through the chunks of celernip and the celernip root. The cupcake tasted a little sweet, but mostly like soggy cardboard. He chewed and chewed the cupcake into smaller and smaller bites until it was all gone.

But nothing happened. He didn't feel sick. He didn't feel too hot or too cold. He didn't feel anything strange happening to him like with all the other cupcakes. Was the cupcake a dud? Was that why his sister had thrown it away? Horace tapped a foot, waiting for something to happen. But nothing did. And the longer he waited, the more people gathered outside Madame Chantilly Bellray's House of Beauty and gazed up at the giant balloon floating in the sky. Auggie and Xax's mom was standing right next to Madame Bellray. Bitty came out of the shop with her wig back on her head and Wiggles at her side.

Horace felt his stomach rumble.

Burp.

He opened his mouth, and a thin celernip dart shot out of his mouth and into the air above the heads of the crowd. The celernip dart flew right into the middle of Madame Bellray's sign and—*poing*—stuck there.

Everyone turned their heads, looked at the Cupacked Crusader, and clapped.

"Our town hero has arrived! Hooray!" a man shouted.

"I love you, Cupcaked Crusader," a little girl said.

Horace felt his stomach growling louder. He felt like he couldn't stop himself and—*burp, burp, burp, burp*—four more celernip darts sprang from his mouth and into the crowd.

"The Cupcaked Crusader is attacking us!" a man shouted.

"My goodness, he's gone mad!" screamed an old woman, covering her face with her handbag.

Horace felt his stomach gurgling. There was

nothing he could do to stop it—*burp, burp, burp, burp—burp, burp, burp, burp—burp, burp, burp, burp*—the burping went on and on and on. Every time Horace burped, another celernip dart shot from his mouth and into the air.

Some popped car tires.

Some cracked store windows.

Some got stuck in people's rear ends.

And others shot into trees, streetlights, traffic signs, and the sale rack hanging outside the Watermelon-Wear, exploding pits and juice all over everybody.

But worst of all, exactly twenty-three darts hurtled high into the sky and shot into the giant balloon that floated right above the crowd.

Kablammo!

The balloon exploded with over one hundred pink butterfly hair clips. The clips sparkled in the sunlight and fell through the air, landing atop all the people's heads who stood outside . . . except the Cupcaked Crusader's.

HAIR-O OR VILLAIN?

Horace clutched his stomach and tried to keep from burping, but it didn't really matter anymore. All the damage had already been done. People were running everywhere as the butterfly clips snapped across their scalps, chewing off all their hair. Boys and girls slapped their hands at the clips, men banged their heads against trees, and women tried to bat the hair clips off their heads with pocketbooks. But nothing worked. Within a matter of thirty seconds, everyone on the ground was bald with a pretty pink butterfly hair clip stuck to the center of their heads.

Horace's stomach calmed down and his

burping stopped. "Uh, don't worry, everyone," he told the crowd of bald people. "I'll make sure I find out who did this so it never happens again."

Men, women, and children stared at Horace with angry red faces.

"*I* know who did this," said a bald man who was covering his head with a newspaper.

Auggie and Xax's mom stepped forward, her bald head bright. "I saw what the Cupcaked Crusader did to my son last week, and now look at what he's done to all of us!" she yelled. "He must want to ruin the Celernip Festival for everyone because he hates celernip!"

"The Cupcaked Crusader is evil!" bald Timothy Scooplink said.

"I hate the Cupcaked Crusader!" bald Radish Grassy said.

"He's not a superhero. He's a villain!" bald Chantilly Bellray shouted.

"Tie him up so he can't ruin the festival!" bald Señorita Papperilli shouted.

"Let's catch him and put him in jail!" Bitty screamed. She held her wig in her hands. "And if someone wants to borrow my wig, I'll lend it to you for twenty dollars an hour."

"I'll take it," one man said.

Mrs. Blootin pointed a finger at Horace. "My husband's mayor of this town, and I'll make sure the Cupcaked Crusader is locked in a deep, deep dungeon underground so he can never bother us again!"

The crowd of bald people cheered and charged at Horace.

Horace didn't have powers to fly or shoot sparks or do anything that a superhero would do to escape, so he did the only thing he could to get away from the crowd—he jumped onto his bike and began pedaling as fast as his legs were able to. "I didn't do it!" he called as he raced away from the angry mob. "I'm the good guy! I'm here to help! I would never do anything evil to stop the Celernip Festival!"

"*He's a liar!*"

"The Cupcaked Crusader is the enemy!"

"Arrest the Cupcaked Crusader!"

Fortunately for Horace, his celernip darts had popped all the car tires on Main Street, so no one could drive after him. He rode over hills and through fields and woods until he made it safely home. He hid his bike in the garage, tucked his outfit in his backpack, and walked into the house to find his younger sister sitting in front of the TV.

Melody looked up at her brother, then pointed at the news show she was watching. On the screen was a photo of the Cupcaked Crusader with a big red *X* drawn through his face. Under the photo were the words WANTED: STALE OR ROTTEN—THE CUPCAKED CRUSADER.

Melody switched off the TV with the remote. "I hope this teaches you not to steal cupcakes out of my trash ever again," she said. She lifted two pink boots with orange tassels from her lap and held them out to her brother. "Now put these on, twinkletoes. It's time you learned your celernip tap dance."

Horace frowned.

Melody stood and tossed the boots at his feet. "And don't even think about saying no," she told him. "You're going to eat the perfect celernip cupcake that I'm working on, then win this pageant. Or else I'll phone the police and tell them you're the Cupcaked Crusader."

Chapter 12

BLOOTINVILLE'S MOST WANTED

As the day passed, things went from bad to worse. Not only did Horace have to practice his celernip dance, but police cars drove up and down every street in Blootinville calling, "Be on the lookout for the Cupcaked Crusader. And always wear a big hat if you come outside."

Mayor Blootin appeared on the TV news and said, "If you see any large Cupcaked Crusader and dodo balloons, run inside and dial B-L-O-O-T-I-N." He also announced that because of the Cupcaked Crusader, there wouldn't be any pink dodo balloons at the Celernip Festival this year.

"We don't want anyone else to get hurt," he said.

Even Horace's own parents were angry at the superhero. At dinner, Mrs. Splattly said, "The Cupcaked Crusader is terrible. I hate that he's made everyone afraid of pink dodo balloons! And poor Chantilly Bellray has lost so many customers because of all the people whose hair was eaten by those clips. She might go out of business just like Kitty Hello did. Kitty Hello was so mean and gave the worst haircuts ever."

"Kitty was a bad haircutter?" Horace asked.

Mrs. Splattly laughed. "She was so bad that she used to shave her own head and paint her hair on," she said.

Dr. Splattly nodded to Horace. "I remember when she cut the back of your mom's hair really, really short and the front so that it stuck straight out in front of her face like a tunnel."

"Don't remind me," Mrs. Splattly said, giving her hair a pat. "I was so thankful when Madame Bellray came to town so I'd *never* have to go to Kitty again."

Horace swallowed a mouthful of celernip goulash. "I guess it's a good thing her twin sister, Bitty, only makes wigs. Haircutting probably doesn't run in the Hello family," he said with a smile.

Dr. Splattly gave Horace a confused look. "Kitty doesn't have a twin sister. When I was about your age, Kitty was in my class at school. She was an only child."

"But I met Kitty's sister, Bitty. She just opened a wig shop where Kitty's salon used to be," Horace explained.

"Whoever she is, I hope she can help all the people who the Cupcaked Crusader made bald," Mrs. Splattly said.

Melody shrugged. "I guess that's the last we'll be seeing of that squirmy little superhero," she said. "The police think he's left town forever."

"Good riddance," Mrs. Splattly said.

Horace ate his meal without saying another word. Had Bitty told him she was Kitty's twin sister or just a relative? He couldn't remember.

Later that night, before going to bed, Horace sat in his bedroom and felt like the loneliest boy in the world. Everyone hated him now. His parents. His best friends. Sara Willow.

He felt terrible that he'd popped the giant balloon over Main Street, but it wasn't his fault he started burping celernip darts. The cupcake was defective. He'd only eaten it because he wanted to help everyone. He could hardly believe that only six days ago, he'd thought the most important thing was to win the Celernip Prince Pageant so Sara Willow could be his Celernip Princess. Now he didn't care whether he was Celernip Prince or not. Being prince was never as important to him as it was to Auggie and Xax.

And now he wished one of them would win and he wouldn't have to be in the Celernip Prince Pageant at all.

Horace reached for the phone on his night-stand and immediately dialed his friends' phone number.

"Hello?" Xax and Auggie answered at the same time.

Horace didn't know what to say. What could he say?

"Is anyone there?" Xax asked.

"Of course someone's there," Auggie told his brother. "The phone rang, so someone had to call it."

"Maybe a ghost called," Xax said.

"That's totally stupid. Why would a ghost use

a phone if he can walk through walls?" Auggie said.

"Maybe he's shy," Xax said. "Sometimes when I'm shy I like to phone instead of visiting someone."

Before the twins got into a fight, Horace decided it was time to speak up, "Uh, hi, guys, it's me, Horace Splattly."

Silence.

Horace continued. "I know you must hate me, but you have to believe I really didn't do any of this. It was all an accident. I ate a defective cupcake my sister threw in the trash and then everything went crazy. I don't even want to be Celernip Prince anymore, but my sister's making me do it or she'll tell the police I'm the Cupcaked Crusader. And I'm sorry about what I said about telling Sara about the notebook and everything. I was just upset and didn't want everyone to make fun of me."

"*Ha!*" Auggie said. "Why should we believe you? How do we know that you and your sister didn't plan all this and make that big dodo balloon so our mom would get bald?"

"We think you and your sister are trying to scare everyone away from the festival," Xax said.

"You think that if fewer families go to the festival, fewer kids will enter the pageant, so then you'll have a better chance of winning," Auggie said.

"But *we're* not afraid of going," Xax said.

"Not one bit," Auggie said.

Horace rolled onto his stomach and spoke into the phone. "But my sister and I didn't do that. Someone's trying to make it look like I'm the bad guy."

"Prove it," Auggie said. "Or we'll have to tell our dad what you did when he gets home tonight."

"You'd turn me in?" Horace asked.

"If we don't, we'd be accomplices and have to go to jail," Xax said. "I read that in a book of laws I found in my dad's library."

"So can you prove you didn't do it?" Auggie asked.

Horace clutched the phone tightly in a fist. What could he tell them? He had no proof yet and wasn't sure where he'd get any. "Uh . . . uh, how about—how about if I prove it to you by the time the Celernip Festival ends? Please just give me one week to find out who did this, and if I can't, I promise I'll turn myself in to the police."

Silence from the other end of the line.

"I swear I didn't do this," Horace pleaded. "You have to let me prove it to you. You know I wouldn't ever hurt you or your mom or anyone in town on purpose. Come on, you know that."

Silence, then Xax said, "Okay, maybe you didn't *really* do it. But it still kind of looks like you did."

"What about you, Auggie?" Horace asked.

"All right," Auggie said. "We'll give you one week, but that's it. And you better not try to win the Celernip Prince Pageant by eating one of Melody's cupcakes either."

"I already told you—I'd never do that," he told the twins. "And once I prove I had nothing to do with the balloons, then you have to take that page about me out of *The Splattly and Blootin Big Notebook of Worldwide Conspiracies*, okay?"

"Okay," both Blootins said.

"Good. Now, uh, I have to figure all this out, so I gotta go." Horace hung up the phone, lay back on the bed, and wrote a list of the things he had to do to keep Auggie, Xax, and Melody from telling that he was the Cupcaked Crusader:

1. *He had to prove to the twins that he didn't send up the balloons so they wouldn't tell their dad.*
2. *He had to eat Melody's special celernip cupcake and win the Celernip Prince Pageant so she wouldn't tell the police.*
3. *He had to NOT eat Melody's special celernip cupcake or use superpowers to help him win the Celernip Prince Pageant so the twins wouldn't tell their dad.*

Horace grabbed his head and held it tight. He felt as if his brain was going to explode out his ears. There was so much he had to figure out, and he had no idea how he was going to do all this. Was it possible? It had to be. Because if he didn't, everyone in town would know that Horace Splattly was the Cupcaked Crusader and want him put in jail for the rest of his life.

Chapter 13

DRESSED AND DISTRESSED: ONE WEEK LATER

"**F**aster! Faster! Faster!" Melody called from the kitchen counter as she iced the cupcake she had just finished baking. "The festival's in three hours, and you're not throwing the baton high enough! Don't forget to take a bite from each end! And stop tugging on the hem of your kilt!"

Horace stood in the middle of the kitchen wearing the ruffled shirt covered with orange celernips and pink dodo birds and a matching skirt. On his feet were the two knee-high pink boots with orange tassels. "I'm not going to wear a dress in the pageant!" he said, stamping a foot.

Melody frowned. "It's not a dress! It's an exact copy of the celernip kilts the Splattly men wore when they first came to Blootinville over one hundred years ago." She reached for the phone. "Don't make me call the police."

Horace sighed and held up the baton with a celernip stuck on each end. "Why can't you give me a break? I think I've gotten pretty good at this. Now I can even eat the celernips while singing *and* dancing. And I really don't want to eat a special celernip cupcake. I'm sure it will upset my stomach if I eat it right before I perform."

"I've worked hard on this cupcake, and you're going to eat it. It's my best one ever," Melody said. "After you eat this cupcake, you'll *definitely* win the pageant, and then Penny Honey will cry all the way home in her stupid chinchilla-fur sneakers."

"But look how good I am at my dance," Horace said.

Melody set the cupcake down on the counter and watched.

Horace tapped his toes on the tile, tossed the baton in the air, did a kick, then slipped and fell on his butt. The baton clattered to the floor beside him.

"You'll *eat* the cupcake," Melody said, picking it back off the counter. "And that's the end of this discussion."

A full week had passed since his phone call to the twins, yet Horace still didn't have any clue who had sent the pink dodo balloons up into the air. He'd found no information on the Internet, no information in the newspaper, and no information on TV. And if he didn't come up with proof fast, in less than twelve hours Auggie and Xax would tell their father that he was the Cupcaked Crusader.

Thanks to Melody's making him practice dancing so much, Horace had barely had time to figure anything out anyway. Whenever he tried to take a break, his sister would pick up the phone and start to dial the police.

And what was the worst about *that* was that Melody was the only one who really *knew* he didn't send up the balloons!

Horace tap-danced over to his sister. "Don't you think you should tell me what power the cupcake has?" he asked.

Melody finished icing and decorating the cupcake, then put it away in a cabinet. "I want it to be a surprise," she said with a sly grin. "Now change back into your regular clothes. I need to iron your kilt and shirt and polish your boots before we head off to the festival. I can't wait to see Penny Honey's face when you win the pageant and crown me your Celernip Princess!"

• • •

Horace sat in front of the TV sipping a celernip soda and thinking that he'd probably be in jail by this time tomorrow. He stared at a news show, hoping someone would announce that the festival had been canceled.

But no such luck. It would go on exactly as planned.

A news reporter came on TV. He stood outside Miss Bitty Hello's Wig Shop, talking to Bitty. Bitty wore a wig made out of half an umbrella, a bunch of old turkey wishbones, and some long pink ribbons.

"So after the Cupcaked Crusader exploded that balloon that made over one hundred people bald, what happened?" the reporter asked Bitty.

Bitty shook her head sadly and said, "Well, I feel terrible about the whole thing. So many people came to me for wigs that I've been busy making them day and night for the last week. I even sold one that looks like a bouquet of yellow tulips to Madame Chantilly Bellray."

Just then the wind blew, lifting Bitty's wig off her head and into the air. The wig maker's totally bald head glowed in the sunlight. "That stupid, stupid wind!" Bitty yelled, chasing after the wig. She frowned at the reporter. "I told you I wanted to be interviewed inside my shop so it wouldn't be windy!"

Horace looked at Bitty's bald head as she

chased after her wig. He kept thinking that something didn't make sense about her, but he couldn't figure out what. He watched as Bitty caught her wig and put it on her head. The pink ribbons dangled in her face.

Where had he seen those pink ribbons before?

Dr. Splattly, Mrs. Splattly, and Melody entered the room. Melody tossed Horace his backpack. "I put your Celernip Prince costume in the backpack along with a special snack for you to eat before you go onstage," she said, giving him a wink.

"Come along, Horace. Let's get going, we don't want to miss anything," Mrs. Splattly said.

Horace pointed at the TV, wanting to figure out what was bothering him about Bitty Hello.

Dr. Splattly picked up the remote and switched the show off. "You can watch TV later. Now it's time for the festival! Aren't you excited?"

"But—but—but—" Horace said, but before he could get another word out, his sister had grabbed his arm and was dragging him to the car.

Chapter 14

THE NOT-SO-MERRY-GO-ROUND

The Splattlys strolled onto the fairgrounds, where the Celernip Festival was well under way. Blootinites roamed the large field, enjoying the day. Many wore celernips in their hair, around their necks, or strung together into belts that they wore around their waists. But the weirdest thing was people's heads. All the people who had been attacked by butterfly hair clips were wearing wigs of different shapes and sizes. Some were made of Styrofoam and shaped like orangutans, walruses, or a pile of snakes. Some were made of plastic that looked like upside-down bowls atop people's heads. And some were made of metal that was twisted and bent into odd,

strange shapes. And whenever someone took off the wig to adjust it, Horace could see the person's bald head with the butterfly clip stuck to the middle of it.

Bitty Hello stood by the side of the field sipping a celernip soda with an angry look on her face.

The Splattlys walked over to her.

"Why are you upset?" Dr. Splattly asked. "Lots of people have your wigs on, and they look great."

Bitty waved her bottle of soda in the air. "I'm just *very* unhappy that we can't have dodo balloons here! The Cupcaked Crusader hasn't been caught, so people are still afraid of those butterfly hair clips," she said.

"There's still plenty of fun things to enjoy at the festival," Mrs. Splattly said.

"Will your twin sister be coming?" Horace asked.

Bitty rolled her eyes and snarled at him, "Why are you saying something so stupid? I don't have a sister." She stormed off and began arguing with a policeman.

Horace watched her. If Bitty had no sister, then how was she related to Kitty?

"I hope I never have to get a wig from her," Mrs. Splattly said.

The Splattlys looked over the fairgrounds. The field was divided into five areas. In one corner were the rides—the BellySicker, the HeadBanger, the BumCrusher, and the merry-go-round. In another corner were the games: the You-Never-Win Ring Toss game, the Win-a-Bad-Prize ball-toss game, and the How-Many-Marbles-Can-You-Fit-in-Your-Nose? game. Another corner of the field had a large selection of celernip foods. In the last corner, kids played Blootinball, the town's official sport, in which all the members of a team dress as the same household appliance. Teams compete with one another to push a giant ball of rice up a hill. The team that gets it to the top of the hill the most times without the ball falling apart wins, and then the losers have to eat all the dirty rice. Right now the Refrigerators were losing to the Hair Dryers one roll to two.

And in the center of all that activity stood the celernip-shaped tent. It was big and round at the bottom, then swooped up to a long column reaching into the sky. Underneath the tent was the stage where the Celernip Prince Pageant would take place later that day.

"Well, we have a bit of time before the contest begins," Dr. Splattly said. "What would you like to do?"

Horace thought he'd like to find out who was making it look like the Cupcaked Crusader had sent up the giant balloons with the butterfly hair clips, but he didn't think he should tell his parents that.

Melody had a different idea. "Rides! Rides! Rides!" she shouted. "I want to go on the BumCrusher!"

Horace kicked a foot at the ground. "I'm still too little to go on the good rides."

Melody tossed her head back. "That doesn't mean I can't go on the rides, does it? Really, Horace, think about someone else for a change. And you're not too little for the merry-go-round. Why don't you and Mom go on that while Dad and I go on the BumCrusher?"

"That sounds like a good plan," Mrs. Splattly said. "I don't like having my bum crushed anyway. What about you, Horace?"

Horace looked over at the BumCrusher. Each person's bottom was held by a big hand that lifted them into the air, spun them upside down, then dropped them into a giant pillow. All the kids and parents on the ride were screaming and laughing. Horace frowned. "I've never had my bum crushed before, so how would I know if I like it?"

"I'm sure you'll grow enough by next year," Dr. Splattly said.

Dr. Splattly and Melody went off to the BumCrusher. Horace looked at the merry-go-round with all the horses moving up and down and the benches for people who didn't want to ride the horses. He didn't see *anything* very merry about the merry-go-round.

Mrs. Splattly looked down at her son. "Want to go on the ride with me?" she asked.

Horace checked to see if anyone he knew was nearby. He didn't see any kids from school, and since it would make his mother happy . . . "Uh, okay, I guess," he said.

Horace's mom handed a woman their tickets. Horace tried to climb onto a horse but couldn't pull himself up, so his mom lifted him, then sat on the horse next to his.

He sat atop his horse, held the strap, but wasn't able to reach his legs down to hook his feet into the stirrups. Horace thought that if he held on to the pole really tight, he'd still be safe even without the stirrups.

Just then, he looked up and saw his science teacher, Mr. Dienow, strolling through the festival eating a fried celernip on a stick. He spotted Horace sitting on the merry-go-round and walked over.

"Hello, Horace," Mr. Dienow said. "Hello,

Mrs. Splattly. I was just noticing that your son's legs don't reach the stirrups on the horse. He might just be too little to sit on the ride alone."

Mrs. Splattly looked at Horace's feet. "Can you reach the stirrups?" she asked. "If you can't, maybe you need to sit on my horse with me."

Horace wished he could point a finger and fly right over and smack Mr. Dienow in the head. He looked at his mother. "I'll be okay," he told her. "I'm holding on real tight."

"He says he'll be all right," Mrs. Splattly told Mr. Dienow. "But thanks for letting us know."

Mr. Dienow walked off and began to speak to the woman who ran the ride. He whispered something in her ear, then pointed to Horace's feet. A moment later, the woman walked up to Horace and his mom.

"I'm afraid your son's too little to sit on the horse alone," the woman said.

"Horace, come up here with me so I can hold you tight," Mrs. Splattly said.

"Awww, c'mon," Horace moaned.

Mr. Dienow stood off to the side, smiling. He took a camera out of his pocket and aimed it at Horace. "Hey, Horace," he said with a grin. "After you get on the horsey with your mommy, I'll take a picture to hang up in the classroom next year."

Horace grimaced and climbed off the horse. His mom reached down and pulled him up to hers.

Click. Dienow snapped a picture.

Horace knew that when all the kids saw the photo, they'd be laughing for hours.

"Attention! Attention, all Blootinites," a voice boomed over the loudspeakers all over the fairgrounds. "This is Mayor A. X. Blootin with a very special announcement. The Cupcaked Crusader has been caught!"

And right before Horace's eyes were two policemen dragging a short guy in a Cupcaked Crusader costume through the fairgrounds.

Chapter 15

THE ALMOST SHORTEST CHAPTER IN THE BOOK

Horace leaped off the carousel and chased after the policemen as they dragged the Cupcaked Crusader to their car.

A crowd of people clapped for the police.

"Thank goodness," said Chantilly Bellray, wearing her new wig. "If more people went bald, I don't think I'd have any more customers."

Horace raced over to the man in the Cupcaked Crusader costume. They were almost exactly the same size. "Who are you?" Horace asked. "Are you the one who sent up those balloons?"

The Cupcaked Crusader turned his head and snorted.

The policemen looked to Horace. "Sorry, kid, but he's refusing to talk, so we're taking him to the station for questioning." The Cupcaked Crusader grunted as the policemen pushed him into the backseat of their squad car.

Horace watched the policemen drive away. Who was pretending to be the Cupcaked Crusader? Who could possibly want everyone in town to lose their hair? He thought for a moment, and only one name came to him: Bitty Hello.

The wigs.

The mean personality.

Something just wasn't right about her.

Could she be the one? But if she was, then who was wearing the Cupcaked Crusader outfit? Bitty was much taller than whoever was pretending to be the Cupcaked Crusader.

A loudspeaker above everyone's heads boomed. "Everyone, please assemble under the tent in the center of the fairgrounds in fifteen minutes. The hundredth annual Celernip Prince Pageant will begin shortly. And because the Cupcaked Crusader has been caught, I'm happy to report that we *will* now be having dodo balloons at the festival!"

The crowd of Blootinites cheered loudly. All except Horace, who was looking around, trying to find out where Bitty Hello might be.

Chapter 16

The 100th Annual Celernip Prince Pageant, Part 1

Mayor A. X. Blootin stood on the stage. The boys who wanted to be Celernip Prince were sitting behind him. Hundreds of people had crowded into the tent to watch. Hundreds of pink dodo balloons floated above their heads. Horace saw his parents and Melody sitting up front beside Principal Nosair, Madame Chantilly Bellray, and Mr. Dienow. Penny Honey rode into the tent on the back of a pink pony. She wore a huge gold dress with fur trim. Everyone applauded except for Melody. She sat on her hands as her face turned red with anger.

Sara Willow was sitting at the front in her new wig that hid her face except for her two brown eyes. She looked very mysterious, like a spy. Horace wondered if he really could win the pageant, so she'd be his Celernip Princess. He hadn't eaten the cupcake like he'd told Melody he would. He just hadn't wanted to. How could he when he'd promised his friends he wouldn't? The cupcake sat in the bottom of his backpack with his Cupcaked Crusader costume.

Horace sat between Xax Blootin and Cyrus Splinter. Xax was dressed as the town bird: a pink dodo. Cyrus wore a shirt and pants made out of green rubber. Horace wore the shirt, kilt, and boots his sister had made for him. He kept his legs crossed so no one in the audience could see his underwear. Auggie sat next to his brother, wearing the same green-and-white leotard he'd worn almost two weeks ago when he came by Horace's with Penny Honey. He also wore a pile of shredded celernip atop his bald head. Six other kids sat onstage hoping to win, too.

"Nice skirt, Horace," Cyrus teased. "After the pageant are you going to have a tea party with your dollies?"

"It's a kilt," Horace told him, then he looked at Xax. Xax was chewing on his lip and counting all the feathers on his costume. Auggie sat perfectly still with his head held high and a bright smile on his face. Neither twin even glanced in Horace's direction.

"I—I think I almost have proof," Horace whispered. "The police caught some guy who was pretending to be the Cupcaked Crusader, so it's almost all figured out."

Xax looked down at his lap and said nothing.

Auggie stared straight ahead with that big smile plastered across his face.

"C'mon, guys, don't be mad at me," Horace said.

"You still haven't proved it," Auggie said out of the side of his mouth. "And are you going to cheat and use special cupcakes to win?"

"Do you have magical special celernips?" Xax asked out of the side of his dodo beak.

Before Horace could answer, the mayor spoke. "Everyone, please take your seats. The One Hundredth Annual Celernip Prince Pageant is about to begin. After we've seen all the contestants perform, we'll hold a vote by secret ballot and announce the winner at the Celernip Ball this evening."

The crowd cheered and hollered.

"And I am proud to say that our first contestant is from my own family. May I now present Auggie Blootin!"

Auggie sprang to his feet and immediately began doing back flips, twists, cartwheels, and handsprings, all while juggling celernips and bouncing them from his knees to his elbows to his head and then rolling them up and down his arms. And while he was doing that, he smiled and sang his celernip song. For a grand finale, Auggie flipped in the air, spelled out all the letters of the word *celernip* with his body, and tossed all three celernips in the air so they smashed into one another and made mashed celernips, which he caught in a bowl and began eating.

The audience cheered wildly. Auggie bowed proudly and took his seat. Horace looked down at his stupid kilt and frilly shirt and boots. How could he ever beat Auggie when all he could do was eat celernips off the end of a baton?

Mayor Blootin announced the next contestant. "Presenting a member of the family in Blootinville who invented the celernip, Cyrus Splinter!"

Cyrus hauled a huge barrel of celernips to the center of the stage. "For my special talent, I'm going to stuff four hundred celernips down my pants while singing my celernip song."

Cyrus reached into a barrel, pulled out a handful of celernips, and began stuffing them into his pants. "One celernip down the pants is fun, is fun, is fun. Two celernips down the pants is more fun, more fun, more fun. Three celernips down the pants is even more fun, more fun, more fun."

Cyrus went on singing his song as he stuffed celernip after celernip in his clothes. The pants stretched out bigger and bigger and bigger until Cyrus's pants were as big as a washing machine. Finally, after half an hour, his pants were so full, they looked like they were about to burst. Cyrus picked up the last celernip. "And four hundred celernips down the pants is the very best thing in the world!" He stuffed the four-hundredth celernip down his pants.

The audience applauded politely. Cyrus bowed, and as he did so, his pants that had been stretched to the limit burst open, spilling celernips all across the stage and into the audience. Cyrus was left standing in nothing but his shirt and a pair of orange underwear decorated with kittens. People began laughing and Cyrus ran offstage.

Horace smiled to himself. "Guess we don't have

to worry about him winning," he said to Xax.

Xax nodded. "Yep, I just hope I don't screw up my performance."

Horace gave Xax a pat on the back. "I bet you'll be fantastic."

Xax shook his head. "I hope so," he said.

"Well, neither of us will look as stupid as Cyrus," Horace replied. "That's something to be happy about."

The mayor stepped up to the podium and announced the next contestant. "Now presenting the younger of my twin boys by exactly four minutes, Xax Blootin!"

"Good luck," Horace told him.

Xax bit his lip and slowly shuffled to the center of the stage, wearing his pink dodo costume and carrying a straw nest filled with thirty-one celernips. "I will, uh, now do my special dance of the dodo while singing my celernip song." He placed the nest on the floor, then sat in the middle on top of the celernips. The kids in the audience giggled.

Xax began singing:

"I'm the celernip-hatching dodo,
I sit on celernips and help them grow.
I flap my wings,
I sing my song,
And wait for hatching day to come along."

Xax stood and flapped his wings while dancing in a circle around the nest and singing:

"My celernips won't hatch, so what
    should I do?
Should I cry to my mother or paint myself blue?
Should I kick my legs in the air or
    fly to Timbuktu?"

Xax did a little kick in the air, but when he
put his foot back down on the stage, he fell off
balance and landed on one of Cyrus's celernips,
crushing it with his big dodo rear end. People
began laughing. Xax's face turned as pink as his
costume, and when he stood, a big splat of celernip was stuck to the middle of his butt. The
audience laughed louder.

Xax bit his lip, sat back in the nest, and continued:

"I'm the celernip-hatching dodo.
I hope they grow into a happy,
*   squawking batch.*
I first found them in a special celernip patch.
And now I think they're ready to hatch."

Xax stood and pointed a wing at the celernips in the nest. The celernips began shaking as if they were eggs about to hatch. And then one of them did! From inside the celernip, a long nose poked its head out, and then a white-and-green miniature aardvark barked at the audience.

The audience cheered and laughed excitedly.

"One celernip-aardvark hatched!" Xax sang.

Another aardvark hatched from a celernip.

"Two celernip-aardvarks hatched!" Xax and the audience sang together.

Mini-aardvark after mini-aardvark hatched from the eggs. The audience sang louder and louder along with Xax until all thirty-one cel-ernips had hatched.

"Thirty-one celernip-aardvarks hatched!" everyone sang. They all applauded Xax, and he bowed and took his seat.

"That was amazing," Horace told him. "How did you do it?"

Xax beamed a huge smile. "I hollowed out the inside of the celernips, then trained all those baby aardvarks to eat their way out from the insides. I think aardvarks like celernips even more than they like ants."

"Really cool," Horace said. He looked down at his baton with the two celernips on each end. "I wish I didn't even have to do this," he told Xax. "Melody is making me do a talent so dumb, there's no way I can ever win."

Mayor Blootin stood at the podium and announced the next contestant. "And here's the shortest fourth grader in Blootinville Elemen-tary, and he'll soon be the shortest fifth grader in all of Blootinville Elementary, Horace Splattly!"

THE 100TH ANNUAL CELERNIP PRINCE PAGEANT, PART 6 (MINUS 4)

Horace forced a smile as he walked to the center of the stage, carrying Melody's baton with a celernip on each end. He could see Melody sitting next to his parents. She had a stern look on her face that said if he didn't do a good job, she'd smack him. "Uh, hi, everyone. This outfit I'm wearing is an exact copy of the kind my great-great-great-great-grandfather wore. Now I'll perform a special celernip song."

At the other end of the front row sat Bitty Hello. Sweat was rolling off her forehead, down her cheeks, and onto her neck. She tapped her fingers on the arms of her chair like she was very nervous and kept dabbing at her forehead and neck with a napkin to wipe the sweat away.

And that's when Horace saw it. On Bitty's neck was a tattoo in the shape of a pig, and on her napkin were smears of the makeup she'd used to cover it.

"Start your song," Melody hissed from the audience. "Get dancing."

Mayor Blootin came over to Horace and patted him on the shoulder. "I guess Horace is a little nervous. Maybe if we give him a round of applause, he'll start his performance."

The crowd began applauding for Horace.

But Horace wasn't paying attention. He kept staring at Bitty Hello.

Why would *Bitty* cover her pig tattoo with makeup?

And why did it look just like the one *her sister* had in the photo on the wall of the Miss Bitty Hello's Wig Shop?

Why would *Bitty* be so angry that there wouldn't be dodo balloons at the festival?

Why would *Bitty* want everyone who went for haircuts at Madame Bellray's salon to lose their hair?

Because *Bitty* Hello wasn't Bitty Hello! The reason Kitty and Bitty had the same tattoo and both had shaved heads and both couldn't cut hair was because they were the same person! Bitty Hello was really *Kitty* Hello! Kitty had come back to Blootinville to get back at Chantilly Bellray for taking all her business. And Kitty wanted everyone to blame the balloons on the Cupcaked Crusader so he'd get arrested and no one would know she made them. And with the Cupcaked Crusader in jail, there would be no one to stop her from doing all her evil deeds.

But who was the Cupcaked Crusader who'd gotten arrested? Horace remembered how the fake Cupcaked Crusader had grunted at him.

He was Wiggles! Kitty had dressed him to be the Cupcaked Crusader so everyone would think they were safe and could have dodo balloons at the festival again! Dodo balloons she could make and fill with her butterfly hair clips!

Horace looked at Bitty in the audience and suddenly remembered where he'd seen the pink ribbons on her wig before. They were the same pink ribbons that had dangled from the balloons at the school.

"Go ahead, Horace," Mayor Blootin said. "If you don't start your performance, I'll have to disqualify you."

Horace looked at Kitty. She kept tilting her head to the top of the tent at the balloons, then she looked down at her lap, where she was holding a small remote control. Her thumb was right over a bright red button.

What should he do? What could he do? He saw Kitty's thumb press the button.

Pop!

One of the dodo balloons floating at the top of the tent popped, dropping a butterfly hair clip on a man's head below. "Help! Help!" he screamed. The clip snapped across his head, made him bald, and stuck there.

Pop! Pop! Pop! Pop! Pop!

More and more balloons popped and released more and more butterfly clips onto people's heads. Horace was so busy watching the balloons popping that he dropped his celernip baton to the stage floor. The bursting of balloons continued. The tent sounded as if it were a giant popcorn machine. People were running everywhere, covering their heads and trying to get out. But before anyone could escape through the opening, it was suddenly blocked by a large truck. It looked as if no one was going to be able to leave the tent with hair on their heads.

Horace dashed behind the stage, pulled out his backpack, and hid behind a curtain. He quickly pulled on his Cupcaked Crusader outfit and took the celernip cupcake Melody had given him from out of the front pocket. He might not have wanted to use powers to win the contest,

but he sure would use them to stop Kitty Hello.

The celernip cupcake was pale green with a shriveled green celernip skin on top and two celernip roots sticking out of the bottom.

Horace could hear more and more popping of balloons and people screaming as the butterfly hair clips ate their hair and stuck to their heads. He knew that if he was going to stop what was happening, he'd have to just eat the cupcake and hope it gave him powers that he needed to help everyone.

Horace stuffed the cupcake in his mouth. Instantly, it exploded with a burst of green smoke that smelled like rotten eggs. Seconds later, he felt two bumps on his forehead. The bumps grew and grew until they poked holes through the costume. Horace touched the bumps. They felt like two mini-celernips sticking out of his forehead.

Horace felt the mini-celernips trying to shoot something, but he couldn't figure out how to make them work. First he pressed them with his hands, then he shook his head back and forth. Nothing happened. He thought really hard, wrinkling his forehead. The mini-celernips instantly shot out a small burst of green fireworks in the shape of a celernip.

Perfect!

Horace knew exactly what he had to do. He ran from behind the stage. Most of the balloons had popped and butterfly clips were eating the hair off people's heads. Some people had no hair left and some had half or most of their hair.

"It's the Cupcaked Crusader! He escaped from the police and is here to hurt us!" Madame Chantilly Bellray yelled as four hair clips snapped at her giant wig.

People pointed at Horace and screamed in panic.

"No, I'm here to help," Horace told them. "Watch." He pointed his mini-celernips at Madame Chantilly Bellray and wrinkled his forehead. Two green fireworks celernips hit all the butterfly clips and blew them off her head.

"The Cupcaked Crusader can save us!" people cheered.

"Help me! Help me!" called a man with a butterfly clip in his hair.

Horace blasted the clip off, and it fell to the ground. Then he pointed the mini-celernips in every direction, blasting the clips off people's heads. He even blasted clips off his mom, his dad, the mayor, and Penny Honey. Melody hid under her chair so none of the clips could get at her head.

"Thank you!" Everyone applauded.

"You won't stop me, you crumbly cupcake!" a woman shrieked. Suddenly one of the entrances to the tent opened, and Kitty Hello entered on the back of a giant silver butterfly hair clip. She flew over everyone's head and aimed the contraption right at Horace.

Horace could see the beast's huge mouth and teeth. If he didn't do something fast, it would eat him in one gulp.

"Don't do it, *Kitty!*" he yelled.

The crowd of people looked at Horace, confused.

Horace pointed at Kitty. "That's not Bitty Hello," he told them. "That's Kitty Hello. She came back to town pretending she was her twin sister. She hated that no one liked her haircutting, so she came back to make everyone bald so they'd have to buy her wigs and drive Madame Bellray out of business. And she tried to blame me so you'd arrest me and then she'd be able to do all her dirty work without anyone stopping her. Well, I couldn't let that happen!"

All the people in town gasped.

Kitty Hello laughed and flew her giant hair clip around the tent. "I knew you were the only one in town with strong enough powers to stop me. And even though I didn't get you put in jail, that doesn't mean I can't put an end to you and make everyone bald!" She aimed her hair clip right at Horace and charged.

Everyone screamed and watched as the giant hair clip's sharp metal teeth snapped open and closed. They were only a few feet from the Cupcaked Crusader.

Horace wrinkled his forehead as hard as he could, and shot a blast of fireworks at the hair clip. They exploded as they reached Kitty. Just like all the other fireworks, this one was in the shape of celernip, but it was much, much, much bigger. And underneath the giant fireworks were giant sparkling letters spelling out the words HAPPY CELERNIP FESTIVAL!

The giant hair clip clattered to the ground. Kitty Hello tried to run away, but the crowd surrounded her and tied her to a pole.

Mayor Blootin stepped onto the stage and clapped his hands. "Everyone, let's thank our hero of the day: the Cupcaked Crusader!"

The crowd applauded. Horace smiled as photographers took pictures for the paper and the TV newscasts. The police came in to take Kitty Hello away, and all the hair clips were tossed into a garbage truck, where they were crushed to bits.

Auggie and Xax rushed over to Horace.

"We're sorry we didn't believe you," Auggie said. "It's just you started being mean about the pageant, so it made us angry."

"Yeah, it was like you cared more about winning this than being our friend," Xax said.

"I know. I'm sorry," Horace said. "I was just sick of everyone picking on me for being little."

"We'll stick up for you more if anyone ever does again, okay?" Auggie said.

"We promise," Xax said.

"Thanks, guys," Horace said.

"And now we'll continue with our Celernip Prince Pageant," the mayor declared. "Please everyone, take your seats and we'll continue."

"Where's Horace?" Dr. Splattly asked. "Horace is gone."

The Cupcaked Crusader said good-bye to Xax and Auggie, then dashed backstage. Now what should he do? Everyone had already seen him with the two mini-celernips on his head as the Cupcaked Crusader, so there was no way he could just change back into his regular clothes and finish his performance as Horace Splattly. He peeked from behind a curtain.

"Can someone find Horace?" Mrs. Splattly asked.

The mayor shouted into the hall. "Has anyone seen Horace Splattly? He's an awfully little boy, so he may be under your seat or in your handbag."

Cyrus Splinter, now wearing a paper bag, pointed to the back of the tent. "I saw him hide behind the stage. I think he crawled out the back of the tent like an itty-bitty baby."

Dr. and Mrs. Splattly took Melody's hands and began walking toward the entrance. "We better go home and see if he's all right," Dr. Splattly said.

"I hope he's not too scared," Mrs. Splattly said.

Melody grimaced. "I guess I won't get to be Celernip Princess," she said.

Horace ducked out the back of the tent and

began running home as fast as he could. The Cupcaked Crusader had saved the day! And even though he wouldn't get to make Sara Willow his Celernip Princess, he didn't care. He'd proven to everyone that the Cupcaked Crusader was a good guy. He'd also let Auggie and Xax know that their friendship mattered more to him than being popular.

But most important of all was what Horace had learned about himself. He now knew that it didn't matter whether he was Celernip Prince or not. After all, why should he care about being Celernip Prince? He was the Cupcaked Crusader!

And being a superhero and helping people in trouble made him feel better than anything else in the world ever could.

AND THE WINNER IS . . .

The celernips sticking out of Horace's head had disappeared by the time he was back at his house and tucked into his bed. When his parents arrived home, he told them that while he was onstage, he had gotten a really bad headache, so he'd rushed home to lie down. He also explained that he was feeling much better, so he'd be able to attend the Celernip Ball that night. Dr. and Mrs. Splattly scolded Horace for running off without telling them, but they were happy his headache had gone away.

Melody waited for her parents to leave the room, then marched up to Horace's bed and wagged a finger at her brother. "You were supposed to eat that cupcake and make the fireworks explode while you were dancing," she said.

"Don't you think I'd look stupid dancing with two celernips attached to my head?" Horace asked.

"No stupider than you usually look," Melody replied. "You're just lucky I'm such a nice sister."

"Well, you can't call the police now," Horace said. "They know it was Kitty Hello's fault and not mine. And if you told that I was the Cupcaked Crusader, then Mom and Dad would know that you made the cupcakes and probably take away all your stuff, so you couldn't do any more experiments on me."

"Well, next year you better stay in the pageant and win," Melody said. "In fact, I'll go start making plans now. We can begin practicing tomorrow." She left the room.

Horace was so tired from all the day's events, he decided not to argue with his sister.

Until tomorrow.

• • •

The night was warm, stars lit the sky, and Blootinites were dressed in their finest clothes and dancing in the town square to the sounds of the One-Song Knitting Quartet. The band was made up of four eighty-year-old women, and they played one song over and over, using violins and knitting needles. The only song they ever played was "The Hokey Pokey," but that was okay because "The Hokey Pokey" was the Blootinville anthem, and everyone loved singing and dancing to it.

Now the whole Splattly family was dancing in a giant ring of hokey pokey dancers. Many of the women and men at the ball had lost all or part of their hair because of the hair-clip attack that afternoon. But thanks to some hard work by Madame Chantilly Bellray, the bald and

partly bald people were now wearing fantastic new wigs and hairpieces. Some men had rings of bright red hair on their heads with bald circles in the middle. Some women who'd had half their hair eaten that afternoon had replaced it with a completely different color so one half was black and the other was white. Mrs. Splattly had the front part of her hair eaten and replaced it with a polka-dotted piece that Madame Bellray made. Penny Honey was missing a small patch from the very top of her head. The hairdresser had given her a special long, curly pink hairpiece to cover it. When Melody saw it, she wished a butterfly hair clip had gotten her so she could have one, too.

And even though everyone was glad that the hair clips were gone, people really liked their wigs and were having a lot of fun with them. Many people said that even if their hair grew back, they'd cut it all off.

After everyone had danced the hokey pokey a few times, the band took a break.

Horace met up with Auggie and Xax and sat down at a table, where they sipped their celernip sodas and ate chocolate-covered celernip on a stick.

"That was pretty amazing what you did this afternoon," Auggie said in a whisper.

"Yeah, pretty Cupcaked Crusader incredible," Xax said.

"Thanks," Horace answered. "I just wish I could have stopped more of those things before they got people."

Auggie finished off his celernip treat and tucked the stick behind his ear. "Sorry you didn't get to be in the pageant."

Horace finished off his celernip treat and tucked the stick behind his ear, too. "I wouldn't have won anyway. The stuff Melody was making me do was really dumb."

"Had to be better than watching Cyrus Splinter stuff celernips down his pants," Auggie said.

"Yeah," Xax said. "The only good part about his performance was the counting."

Mayor Blootin stepped onto the bandstand in front of the townspeople, holding an envelope. "Attention, everyone. In this sealed envelope is the name of this year's Celernip Prince."

Everyone stood silently. The only sound that could be heard was the grunting of Kitty Hello's pet, Wiggles. He'd been released from the town jail earlier that day and now sat on Madame Bellray's lap, wearing a shiny silver wig and grunting as he ate a bowl of peanut butter and celernips.

Mayor Blootin tore open the envelope. "The One Hundredth Celernip Prince is . . . Xax Blootin!"

Xax leaped out of his seat. "It's me? Me?"

"Yowee-zowee-zooks!" Horace cheered.

Auggie gave his brother a hug. "Congrats, twin. You deserved to win. I thought you were the best."

Xax smiled and walked up to the podium. Mayor Blootin crowned Xax with a golden crown that looked like a celernip. Everyone cheered.

The One-Song Knitting Quartet began play-
ing "The Hokey Pokey."

Mayor Blootin leaned down to his son. "It's
time to choose your Celernip Princess and
dance," he told him.

Horace watched Xax to see who he would
choose. Xax walked down from the bandstand
and wandered through the crowd as the music
played. He finally reached out and took his
mother's hand and led her to the center of the
dance floor. Mrs. Blootin wore a wig that was in

the shape of a celernip; standing on top of it were miniature dolls of her husband and two boys.

"The Celernip Prince has chosen," Mayor Blootin announced. "This year's Celernip Princess is Mrs. Serena Blootin!"

Xax and his mom began doing the hokey pokey for the crowd, and everyone applauded.

Horace laughed and turned to Auggie. "Maybe you'll win next year," he said.

Auggie nodded. "Yeah, maybe. I'm glad he won, though. He did it all on his own without anyone else's help."

"He does deserve it," Horace agreed. He looked across the town square at Sara Willow. She was wearing a dress made out of hundreds of strands of pink spaghetti and a wig that was made of hundreds of kernels of pink popcorn. "You know what? I'm thinking that maybe next year I'll enter the pageant and do it on my own. Then I could make Sara my Celernip Princess, huh?" he asked.

"Maybe," Auggie said. "Or maybe you'll like someone else by then. Do you think that could happen?"

Horace looked at Sara Willow again. Could he like someone else by next year? "I don't think so," he told Auggie. "But I guess we'll just have to wait and see."

"Do you have any ideas about what problem the Cupcaked Crusader should solve next?" Auggie asked.

Horace wrinkled his brow. "Hmm . . . I'm not sure, but tomorrow you, me, and Xax can look in *The Splattly and Blootin Big Notebook of Worldwide Conspiracies* and figure it out. Maybe we can explore Lake Honkaninny for that giant bee with five eyes," he said.

"That would be great," Auggie said.

The four old ladies started up "The Hokey Pokey" for the fifty-ninth time.

Horace smiled. "Care to hoke and poke a bit?" he asked Auggie.

"Sure, that's what we're here for," Auggie said.

The two friends joined the giant circle with Xax, Mrs. Blootin, Mayor Blootin, Dr. and Mrs. Splattly, Madame Bellray, Wiggles, Melody, and everyone else in town. They put their right feet in, their right feet out, their right feet in, and shook them all about.

Horace smiled at Auggie and Xax. "Do you think I'm the only superhero ever who did the hokey pokey to celebrate catching a villain?" he asked.

"Definitely," Auggie said.

"Absolutely," Xax said.

The boys all laughed and stuck their right hands in, out, in again, then shook them all about.

Because that's what being a good Blootinite was all about.

And because that's what even the most serious superhero had to do when he wanted to have fun and be silly with his friends.

Lawrence David is 103 years old. He was a superhero for many years and had the power to eat lots and lots of candy bars without ever getting sick. Now he writes books and lives in New York City with his seven pet porcupines, named Radish, Macaroni, Wally, Simon, Sunshine, Persephone, and Dandelion.

Barry Gott is younger, but not by much. Although he has spent much of his life trying to bake superpower-giving cupcakes, the only superpower he's gotten is the ability to play the tuba and yodel at the same time. He has illustrated two other books about Horace as well as several picture books. He lives with his family, but no porcupines, in Ohio.